WATCH YOUR BACK

BOOK TWO, VOLUME TWO
Published by KY Lewis 2024

WATCH YOUR BACK

Summer Meadows Cozy Mystery series, Volume 2

KY Lewis

Published by KY Lewis, 2025.

This is a work of fiction. Similarities to real people, places, or events, are entirely coincidental.
WATCH YOUR BACK
First edition May 31,2024
Copyright @2024 KY Lewis
Written by KY Lewis

This is a work of fiction. Similarities to real people, places, or events are entirely coincidental.

WATCH YOUR BACK

First edition. January 31, 2025.

Copyright © 2025 KY Lewis.

ISBN: 979-8230001270

Written by KY Lewis.

Table of Contents

WATCH YOUR BACK (Summer Meadows Cozy Mystery series, #2) 1
PROLOGUE 3
PROLOGUE 6
1 7
2 10
3 14
4 16
5 18
6 21
7 23
8 26
9 27
10 30
11 34
12 39
13 43
14 45
15 48
16 51
17 56
18 58
19 61
20 64
22 67
23 69

Dedicated to God, family and friends!

I wanted to thank God first for always being there. Thanks Momma for giving me feedback through my writing process. This series is dedicated to my parents. I want to thank the rest of my family and friends for their support as well
.

PROLOGUE

1

2

3

4

5

6

7

8

9

10

11

12

13

14

15

16

17

18

19

20

21

22

PROLOGUE

As Jessica stumbled a bit walking back to her car in the den parking lot, she thought she heard footsteps behind her. Jessica had just come from a nightclub called DJ's in White Oak Mississippi. She was having a girls' night out with Summer, Cheyenne and Ruby Jean. She had just moved back to Blue Ashe and wanted to catch up with old friends. The sounds of the footprints started echoing louder behind her. Jessica was too frightened to turn around and look.

She whispered to herself, "I really should have left with the three of them!"

She felt and heard someone's warm breath whisper "Jessica" into her right ear. This made the hairs on the back of her neck stand up.

The killer smirked and said, "Yes you should have gone home with the three witches!" then
chuckle to themselves. That's when everything went black for Jessica.

1

The next morning I was going to meet Cheyenne, Ruby Jean and Jessica at the Breakfast Bar Coffee Shop here in Blue Ash. I walked through the coffee shop doors to see Ruby Jean and Cheyenne sitting at a table. I took a seat at the table. They had already ordered me my favorite latte and blueberry bagel with cream cheese. I looked at the empty chair next to me where a coffee and bagel were at the table.

I said, "where is Jessica?" Tilting my head to the left. There was a strange pause between all three of us.

"She's probably hungover. I saw her talking with that dorky Pete guy at the club last night. Cheyenne almost choked on her coffee. We looked at each other and smirked.

" Well, right, Ruby Jean, he's the dork? I can't believe she's not here yet, maybe she forgot? Let me call her." When I called Jessica's phone it just went to voicemail. Cheyenne's phone rang.

"Hey Jay."

" Cheyenne can you, Summer and Ruby Jean come down to the station. I have some bad news?" Jay told her.

"Sure but what's going on? Can't you tell me something over the phone?"

"Under the circumstances it wouldn't be appropriate to talk about it on the phone."

"Okie dokie, be right there."

" Ladies, Jay wants us to come down to the police station and he won't tell me why."

"Oh my word, what if they found a body! I better call Jonathan and make sure he's still alive!" Ruby Jean's eyes widened and her lips scrunch up.

Cheyenne and I just shook our heads. Ruby Jean always says something funny that makes us want to laugh. We love her.

We all headed out for the police station. Jay asked us to come into his office and shut the door. Cheyenne leaned up against the wall and Ruby Jean and I took a seat. Jay took a deep breath and that made us want to hold our breath.

"All right ladies I have some bad news. A lady's body was found in the dumpster at the DJ's Nightclub in White Ashe. The lady was identified as Jessica Barlow. I'm sorry ladies."

We all looked at each other's shocked.

Ruby Jean spoke up, "I knew it! I'm glad I called Jonathan because he said he's still alive!"

Jay cleared his throat, ok right, Ruby Jean it wouldn't be Jonathan because the body is a female and it was Jessica Barlow!

"Oh Jessica, we had so much fun last night and she wasn't dead." Ruby Jean looked confused.

"Poor Jessica, she was in great spirits last night. It's been two years since the Tick Tock killings!" Cheyenne commented while tearing up.

"I don't know what to say, I can't believe Jessica's gone. We should have made her leave with us!" I thought "Ugh, I really don't want to think about the Tick Tock game. It's still scary to think about Sabrina being my own twin and a killer!" I squirmed in the chair and my eyes watered.

Jay's office door opened and Jonathan walked in.

"Hey Big Mama!" Jonathan said to Ruby Jean.

"Hey my hunky man!" Ruby Jean said to him as she puckered her lips.

"Jay I just came over to let you know I'm not dead!"

Jay cleared his throat which he does when he's either irritated or uncomfortable.

"Well thank you Jonathan, I'm glad you're not dead." Cheyenne and I would normally have snickered but this was too tragic.

"Baby, it was Jessica Clark who was murdered," Ruby Jean commented.
"Oh no you're kidding me! That is terrible. Poor Jessica!" He shook his head. "So who is Jessica Barlow?" He has a confused look on his face.

Jay cleared his throat, shut his eyes and scratched his head. Sometimes he doesn't know how to deal with Ruby Jean and Jonathan.
"She's the one that we went out with last night honey." Ruby Jean half smiled.
Oh okay, I'm glad we're all still alive here! Cool, I got to get back to work."

Jonathan abruptly walked out and left.

After getting our account of last night, Jay said "All right ladies, I want you to be on high alert, watch each other's backs and watch your own back. Be aware of your surroundings. Lock doors and windows. Please try to stay safe. We don't need any more killings. I'll be devastated if something were to happen to you ladies. You ladies can go now. Please take heed to my advice. Summer, could you please stay behind for a moment?"

I stayed seated while Cheyenne and Ruby Jean left.

"Summer, are we still going to go on a picnic next Saturday?" I hesitated because I was trying to process Jessica's murder.

" I guess that would still be ok. It might get my mind off Jessica for a while."

"I agree Summer that's the reason I brought it up."

"Ok and you know I'm going to grill you on Jessica's case. She was our friend. See you soon."
Jay rolled his eyes at me as I was walking out the door. He hates it when any of us play detective.

✶✶

I GET HOME AND I'M greeted by Augie so I love him. Mr Stew is on his post curled up in a ball sound asleep.
I got a text from Wyatt. "Can you come in and train the new girl Monday morning instead of working the night shift? Addison won't do
it even though she is working the day shift."

" Sure no problem!"

The rest of the day I took a nap and got things done around my condo until bedtime. I watched some TV and went to sleep with Augie and Mr. Stew at the foot of my bed.

ROLLING INTO SUNDAY I met everyone at church. Cheyenne and Jay were sitting in the back row with Ruby Jean and Jonathan. I sat down next to Jay. Billy came in after me and sat next to Cheyenne. The service was wonderful. We all decided to go to lunch. The shop was closed on Sundays and Jay and Billy don't work on Sundays.

We were all enjoying lunch when Jonathan brought up Jessica.
It seemed we all took a deep breath.
" Her viewing is Tuesday 4pm. to 8pm.The funeral is just family."

"Ok, myself, you and Ruby Jean can go together. Billy, you know her if you want to go?

"I'm good. I never was a fan of hers." "Billy, be nice!"
Billy rolled his eyes.
"We get mean text . Someone is mad at us Jay!" Ruby Jean states.

"I know, heed to my instructions I gave you three the other day. If you get a text, don't engage." Jay was stern.
I thought to myself, " Oh, I will engage. I will tell them off. They make my blood boil!"
Everyone was done eating and went home. Jay came back to my place to binge watch movies. We ordered a pizza. At bedtime I went to bed with Mr. Stew and Augie at the foot of my bed. Jay slept on the sofa.

MONDAY WHEN I PULLED into the shop parking lot, I saw Cheyenne standing at the side of the building looking at her phone. When I got out of my car she stuffed her phone in her back pocket.

"Hey!" she said.

I could hear Cheyenne's phone vibrate and she took it out of her back pocket. Her screen was so good and I could see briefly that it said

"I'm not sure when that'll happen, but that could be when." She shoved her phone into her back pocket again.

"Let's go in," she says as she starts to walk towards the front.

I think to myself, "Okay that was weird."

Little did I know her and Jay were having a private conversation back and forth that had to do with me.

I grabbed my equipment bag and phone out of my car. I headed inside.

2

All the stylists are still here except of course Callie. First person I saw was Addison standing at her station looking in the mirror. I can see her glare at me. She still hates me, but even more so now. You see, Jay and I had gotten back together and that burns Addison up even till today! Jay and I have a bond that cannot be broken and we were always meant to be together. I had denied it for a long time. The next person I see is Wyatt who nodded his head.

" THANK YOU FOR COMING in for a few hours. Look for everything while you're training her, please."

I knew what he meant, she is fresh out of school. I need to check her work. Wyatt is pleasant these days. Can you believe it? He ended up marrying Beverly, but he does miss Dottie. We all missed judging him when he was married to Dottie. He actually did love her. Beverly really helped him get over his grief and they're both happy together. I guess Wyatt loves older women. Cheyenne and the new girl Bailey walked up from the back.

"Hi Bailey, I'm Summer the assistant manager and I'm going to be training you for a few hours. After each service you do I'm going to need to check it. This should only be for a few hours if everything runs smoothly."

"Okay cool." Bailey smiled.

Beau came through the front door.

"Hey y'all I'm here let's get this party started!" He chuckles a little and then stops when he sees Bailey.

"Hum, and who are you little Miss Muffet?"

"Quit being spicy, Beau. This is our new girl Bailey." I answered.

He scrunched his nose at me and said sarcastically, "Ok!"

Right then both Cheyenne's phone and my phone dined. We both get a message from a private number.

"You three witches are nosey. You had better watch your back!"

We both looked at each other and rolled our eyes.

"I sure hope we are not going to have a repeat of two years ago!" Cheyenne uttered.

"I hope not!" I blew air out of my lips.

" Hey, leave us alone!" Ruby Jean responded to the creeper.

He must have included Ruby Jean in the text. I wonder who else he included.

" Never witches!"

It was about 2:00p.m. when Billy walked through the doors.

He was here to pick Cheyenne up. They are back together as well.

"What's up everyone?" He says announcing himself. I show Billy the text.

"It's probably somebody just trying to scare you ladies." Billy shrugged his shoulders.

"I hope so Billy!" I sigh.

" I'm almost ready Billy."

Cheyenne was finishing packing up her stuff. When she was done they left. Wyatt went ahead and left also.
Now it's myself, Bailey and Addison. Beau is out back smoking. I went to the back and grabbed a few towels. As I approached the corner to come back up front I could hear Addison and Bailey talking.

"My family owns the shop so you want to stick with me. Summer is a backstabber and she stole my boyfriend. She is definitely not trustworthy!"

I chucked to myself about how petty Addison can be. I guess she wants to turn Bailey into another Callie since she doesn't have any other friends.
A regular client named Roger came in.

"Hi Roger, Bailey will be cutting your hair today. You can have a seat in her chair."

" So you're the new girl?" Roger smiled at Bailey.

She smiled shyly and said "Yes."

I had her go ahead and start the hair cut. She was all over the place. I had to stop her right away and show her what she was doing wrong.

"Bailey, you need to have a guide through the whole haircut. You can't be all over the place or you will have patch

work or uneven issues all over the head."

Roger remained quiet because he is laid back. Beau on the other hand came right up behind us.

"Girl, didn't they teach you that in school? I mean, it's the basics. Seriously, how did you pass the state board to get your license?"

"Beau, stop!" I barked at him.

" Summer I'm just... Fine, don't expect me to clean up her messes.

I ain't got time for that."

With hands on my hips, I stare Beau down.

" Ewe, ok, Miss Summer giving me a look? I'm going, I'm going. If looks could kill I'd be dead right now!" Beau smirked.

Addison laughed while Bailey got teary eyed.

"Little Miss muffet,you're going to have to get thicker skin if you are going to be in this business. The public can be brutal! No offense Roger." Beau winked at Roger.

"Hey man, I'm good. "Roger smiled.

At 4:00 p.m. I walked to my car to find a smiley face stick pen shoved in my left front tire. My tire is flat as can be.

"Seriously!" I threw my hand in the air.

I got another text. " It should have been you that died, not your sister! I hope you enjoyed my smiley face."

"Bug off you loser! My sister was crazy and so are you!

Now, go away!", I text.

"You and your two witches wish I would go away. I think

it's time for someone to die."

I could feel my left jaw tightening up and my blood pressure climb.

" You psycho leave me alone!"

" Ha-ha the queen bee Summer Meadows is upset! Until next time! Remember, watch your back!"

I called Jay and told him what happened. He came and got me. He had one of his officers fix my tire while we went to an early dinner. We were enjoying each other's company when Jay got a call from Billy.

" Hey man, I have bad news. Mrs. Betty found Rhett dead

at the bottom of the stairs."

"Aww, man! Ok Billy, Summer and I will be there soon." Jay hung up.

"What is it Jay?"

"How do I say this? Your Aunt Betty found Rhett dead at

the bottom of the stairs."

" Jay, I have to get to Aunt Betty's house right away! She must be frantic!"

Tears started well up in my eyes and my stomach became nauseous.

3

We arrived at Aunt Betty's place. There are two cop cars, an ambulance and the coroner. We get out and I pause to take a deep breath.

"Jay, I have to be strong for Aunt Betty. I'm just taking a moment here to breathe and collect my thoughts."

I bent over holding on to my knees taking in another deep breath.

" Ok, I'm ready, let's go in."

I follow Jay into the house and see Aunt Betty sitting on the couch. She has her face in her hands and she's wailing. I give her a warm hug and sit down next to her. Jay went over to speak with the coroner and take a look at Rhett.

"Hey Jay, so we meet again. This is starting to look like a pattern that happened 2 years ago."

Jay took a deep breath. "Yeah, it's starting to look like it. So are you positive this was a homicide?"

"I'm almost 100% sure. He was either pushed or tripped. I can tell by the damage done and the position of the body.

An autopsy will tell me for sure! I will let you know."

I was sitting there with my Aunt Betty comforting her when my phone dings. It's another text from the killer.

" It was so easy to push Rhett down the steps. He didn't even see me come up behind him. I almost felt guilty for a moment because it was so easy to push an old man down

the steps. Who will be next?"

My phone dinged again twice and it was Cheyenne and

Ruby Jean.

" Did you just get that psycho's text? Is it true Rhett is

gone?" Cheyenne texted.

Ruby Jean texted, "That text made me sad. Your uncle

Rhett was such a kind man."

"He sure was and my Aunt Betty is a mess!"

"Ruby Jean is right, your uncle was a kind man, he didn't deserve this. I'm sorry Summer." Cheyenne commented.

"Aww, thank you ladies I'll talk to you later."

I took Aunt Betty by the hand.

"I'm here for you, Aunt Betty, whatever you need."

"Summer, I feel so guilty. I should have been here. I thought it'd be okay to go out of town to visit my cousin. You know Rhett doesn't like going out of town, so he stayed here."

"Aunt Betty, this is not your fault! I'm going to go talk to Jay to find out a little more information."

I got up and walked over to Jay and Nancy.

"Jay I got a text from the killer!"

I handed Jay my phone and he read it.

"Ok when any of you three ladies get a text from the killer you need to forward it to me so I can make screenshots. This is proof that your uncle was murdered! Do you have the other text?"

" Yep I saved them."

"Okay, great, send them to me. Last time this happened I didn't have you send the text to me and I really should have. I'm going to start a file.

4

Jay took me back home and we sat on the sofa. Mr Stew laid on the back of the sofa. Augie jumped up in our laps to be petted.

" Jay, tomorrow is Jessica's funeral."

"Do you want me to go with you?"

"That would be nice!"

"Okay, I will go home and pack clothes for tomorrow and

then I'll stay here tonight on the sofa."

It's Tuesday and the funeral went smoothly until we got to the cemetery. We all walked up to the plot where we noticed a rather large bouquet of black roses sitting on a stand.

"Seriously!" I was fuming I could feel my face turning red.

Jonathan speaks up. "Y'all we didn't send those black flowers! I'm not superstitious, but black roses are spooky!"

"Jessica's mother started to cry again when she saw the roses. Myself, Ruby Jean and Cheyenne tried to comfort her for the next couple of hours. Jay brought me home. I laid down for a nap then there was another text from this creep. "Roses are red, violets are blue, I will send Black roses to your funeral too."-Unknown

"Who are you, freak?" - Addison

" Apparently Addison was added to this group text." I think to myself.

"Just get a life you loser!" -Addison

"Addison, don't engage, that is what they want!" I text.

I thought to myself, " I know I said I would engage myself, so I shouldn't be telling her not to engage. She sounds like

a little high school kid so she should stay quiet."

"Oh my word are you the one that killed my

Rhett? You should be ashamed of yourself." -Aunt Betty

"Aunt Betty you're on here as well?" I text.

"I sure am dear."- Aunt Betty

"What is going on here, why am I being bombarded with text?" text- Billy

"Billy you too!" I text.

" Yes Summer I'm here too and this is really irritating because I'm trying to get things done!"-Billy

"Y'all, I just looked at my phone. Now wait a hot minute, what in the blaze is going on here? I ain't got time for this hee haw nonsense!"- Jonathan

"Um, hey Jonathan." I text

"Baby calm down!" -Ruby Jean

"This has really gotten out of hand!" -Cheyenne

"Cheyenne, I agree with you." I texted.

"All right, listen up, this is Jay! I want everyone to stop responding to this fruit loop because that's exactly what they want you to do. The more you engage the more they're entertained,so stop!" -Jay

" Wow Jay is such a big bad sheriff! Who is next on my list to go?" -Unknown

"Do not engage! Anyone!" -Jay

"Hey buddy I don't know who you are harassing everyone! I've got a shotgun with your name all over it. Come and get some

coward!" - Jonathan

"Jonathan I see you're as dumb as Ruby Jean.

You had better listen to your big bad sheriff and not challenge me. I might stick you at the top of my kill list!"- Unknown.

"Ok, enough is enough! If anyone else decides to engage with this nut Job then you will be arrested, period! I am making a record of this whole conversation."-Jay

5

Hours later and I'm ready to go to sleep. I don't wake up around 9:00 a.m. when I get ready for work and feed Mr.Stew and Augie .Mr Stew was staring at his plate thinking to himself.

"Ugh, must it be chicken Pate again? I would like some fish!"

Then he started to eat his breakfast.

" So spoiled" I say to myself and then chuckle.

I headed out the door for work. When I pull into the shop parking lot my favorite spot is open. I grab my stuff and go in. Right away I noticed Mrs.Thompson, a regular client crying and picking up pieces of her hair from her head. She is sitting in Bailey's chair. Apparently Beau was out back taking a smoke break instead of keeping an eye on Bailey.

I put my stuff on my station and went over to Ms. Thompson. She had foil in her hair and pieces of her hair were coming off in clumps. I take her to the shampoo bowl and remove the foil to shampoo her hair right away. The hair is definitely coming out in larger clumps than I thought. I put a conditioning treatment in her hair and let her sit for 10 minutes. Then I walk back over to Bailey.

"Bailey, I know you use bleach. What developer did you use?"

"I mixed 40 volume developer and the bleach. For 45 minutes on her head."

" Why would you use a 40 volume developer with bleach? Especially since she's already a blonde! You should never mix 40 volume developer with bleach! All that does is destroy the hair. Her hair is falling out because you went for 45 minutes with something on her head that destroys the hair. Again, she's already blonde so it doesn't make sense to use these combinations!"

"Ohhh! I thought it would lift brighter because she

wanted it to look even lighter. I'm sorry!"

" Well Bailey, it definitely is brighter, it looks completely white!"

"Again I'm sorry can we put a toner on it so it won't look so white?"

"No, I would not even touch her head for at least a month. What hair she has left is very fragile now. It needs a break from anything. I'm sorry to do this; but for now you can't do any chemicals unless you're being supervised by someone else. Now go ahead and rinse Mrs. Thompson and comb hair out with a wide tooth comb, gently!"

While I was setting up my station she was combing out Ms. Thompson's hair.

" Look at my hair young lady, you destroyed it!

It's coming out in chunks! Where did you get your license from a cereal box?"

I turned around to see Beau sitting in his chair. His eyes got really big when he took a look at Miss Thompson's head. His mouth dropped open. I gave him a look to make sure he wouldn't say anything. He shut his mouth and lifted his right eyebrow as he looked at me. Beau gave me a sarcastic smirk before I looked away.

I quietly mouthed to Beau, " you should have been up here!"

I walk over to Bailey. "Bailey, go ahead and take a small break."

She headed back to the break room with tears in her eyes. Unfortunately I could see bald spots on Mrs. Thompson's head.

"Mrs. Thompson, you're one of our valued clients; so I'll give you a free haircut for a year to try to make up for this!"

"Oh Summer, I really do appreciate that! I don't want anyone else touching my head except for you. That young lady must have gotten her license from a cereal box!"

Beau started to laugh. When I told him to quit laughing he laughed even harder. That actually put a little bit of a smile on Mrs. Thompson's face.

"Ok Mrs. Thompson, come back and see me in about 4 weeks."

"I sure will, maybe I will get enough nerve to cut it all off and start fresh."

I shook my head yes at her and then she left.

Unfortunately I had to write Bailey up. So I took her to my office.

"Bailey I'm sorry but I have to write you up. You can do training with me or whoever I assign you per shift. When I think you're ready, you can do chemicals again.

"How long will that be? I need to make money while I'm here." Bailey got snippy.

I could feel my eyes widening in Surprise. "Bailey, it will take as long as it takes. You should be thankful that you still have a job. I could have fired you over this incident!"

"Summer you didn't have to write me up over this. I mean seriously can't you just teach me and not write me up. It doesn't seem fair!"

"Yes Bailey I did! One I have to justify why I'm giving a client free haircuts for a year. Two, Mrs. Thompson is a great client and I want to keep her as a client."

Bailey turned around and stomped all the way back to her station.

I called Beverly and filled her in on what just happened. I let her know that I will be giving Ms. Thompson a free haircut for a year. Bailey will be supervised by whoever is assigned to her on her shift. Everyone has to help or they will get written up. Beverly was more than happy to approve everything. She actually is really great

and just lets me run the shop the way I need to. I think that's another reason Addison hates me. I went ahead and sent a mass text to everyone.

6

Down at the police station Jay has a new guy starting. His name is Tommy. Tommy hasn't been out of the academy very long. He gave Jay a ride back to Blue Ash when Jay was kidnapped years ago. Jay told Tommy he would give him a job.

"Hey Tommy. Come on into my office. We can talk a little

while you're filling out your paperwork." Jay smiled at Tommy.

They went into Jay's office and had a seat.

"Tommy, would you like something to drink while you're filling out your paperwork?"

"I'm alright man, thanks."

"Cool, now let's get down to business. You will work some days and some nights to get a feel for everything. Now, I have to let you know there is some tension in town. We have someone stalking people I care about and we've had two murders. Guess what I'm telling you is watch your back and stay on your toes."

"Oh wow, no doubt Jay. I'll keep on edge."

"Good, good, glad to hear that. A guy named Billy is second in command. He will be here soon and I will have you

shadow him for the day."

" Okay, cool, I'm ready. I have wanted to be a police officer

since I was 8 years old."

Billy opened up the office door.

"Hey man, you must be Tommy? It's good to meet you." Billy shook hands with Tommy.

"All right buddy, ready to hit the road? The first stop is a coffee shop."

Jay started to chuckle "You and your blueberry danishes, man."

"It's tradition!" Billy replied with a shrug.

Jay smirked at Billy and raised his right eyebrow.

Billy and Tommy headed out to the coffee shop. "So Jay had mentioned you have a killer on the loose!"

"Yeah, it's some crazy stuff. We've had two victims so far. Jessica grew up here then moved away. She just came back. She was out having drinks with Summer Jay's girlfriend, Cheyenne, who's my girlfriend, and Ruby Jean. They left and she wanted to stay, well you can figure the rest out. The other is Summer Meadows's uncle."

"Wow Billy, sounds like it's gotten crazy around here! I grew up in White Ash. I've been living out of town for the police academy. Now I'm back.

Billy shook his head ok.

7

The rest of the week I stayed busy. Now it's Saturday and I can't wait to go on a picnic with Jay. Doing something fun might get my mind off my uncle's funeral that's Monday. There have been too many funerals lately. I went ahead and laid everything out and I even brought a nice bottle of wine.

"Summer, I love you. I'm really sorry you were going through a mess again. I honestly can't figure out who this person is or why they're so angry with this town! This is just a quiet little community."

"Jay, you know I love you as well. I can't figure out who this person is either and what their motive is."

We went ahead and started to eat our food and sip on some wine.

Jay thought to himself, "this seems like a good time to propose to Summer."

He put his hand in his pocket to feel the ring box.

My phone rang and it was Ruby Jean.

"Guess what Summer, Jonathan proposed to me. I'm getting married, woohoo!"

"Oh, Ruby Jean, that is awesome. I'm so happy for you both!"

"Thanks summer, I have a few more people to call. So bye! She hung up.

I chuckled and said "she's so silly."

"Was it some good news?"

"Jonathan just proposed to Ruby Jean and she is very excited."

Jay smiled " nice."

He thought to himself, "I guess I won't be proposing today!"

Jay sent a quick text to Cheyenne letting her know the proposal won't be today. An hour later she still hadn't responded back. This was unusual for her but he decided to go ahead and blow it off. He figured she was just busy with a client.

We just sat and talked and people watched. It was nice.

Then I got a text from Wyatt.

"Hey summer, have you talked to Cheyenne? She did not

show up for her shift!"

"I haven't talked to her since yesterday morning. I will try to reach her."

"Cool thanks!"

"Jay, Cheyenne did not show up for her shift."

Jay raised his right eyebrow. Then he tried to call Cheyenne but got no answer.

"Let's head to her place."he had a concerned look on his face.

So we left and headed to her place.

When we pulled up to the parking space to her condo, we saw no lights on. Jay took out the spare key to her condo that she gave him and opened the door. We were right it was pitch Black in there with no lights on at all. I turn the front room light on. As soon as I did I saw Cheyenne's purse and car keys sitting on the coffee table. We started to look around and Jay went to Cheyenne's bedroom. Her bed looked like it had not been slept in. Cheyenne was nowhere to be found.

Jay let out a sigh and said, "Summer,this is not good. Let me call Billy."

He called Billy who said he hadn't spoken to her since yesterday morning.

Now Jay and I both started to panic. I started calling around asking if anyone had spoken to her but no one had.

Jay took a deep breath.

"Okay let me get my head on straight and do my job"

Billy had rushed over here in a panic.

"Cheyenne and I were supposed to go to the movies after she got off work. I sent her a text and got nothing back. I

figured she was busy with the client."

"Okay Billy, we need to get more officers and trace back to every place that she goes to. There are woods behind these condos. Let's get some canine units out there."

"Jay, I want to help. What can I do?"

"Honestly, my love, the best thing you can do is to hang out and keep your phone on. you can also double check to make sure you have talked to everyone."

" Billy, go ahead and let Tommy know we're going to need his help."

They both headed out. I text Wyatt to let him know what's going on. He wanted to know if there's anything he could do. He also informed me that he has been making Addison train the other new girl I hired because the shop is growing so much. The other new girl's name is Lisa and she's been in the field for 5 years. I heard knocking at the door and Ruby Jean and Jonathan came in and sat down.

"Did they find Cheyenne yet?" Ruby Jean's eyes are wide open.

"No Ruby Jean I'm afraid they haven't! But I think we all should say a prayer and be in agreement." I led a prayer.

Shortly I got a text. "I see you're missing a person! Don't worry she is safe, at least for now.

8

I could feel my blood pressure rising and I was getting hot. I couldn't say anything about the text because Billy just came back through the door. He looked defeated. I felt like it would be better just to wait and show the text to Jay. "You ok Billy?"

"No Summer I'm not. Not until we find my little lady."

Jonathan spoke up."Hey man, I want to help in the search."

"Sounds good, let's go into the woods with flashlights. The K9 unit could miss something."

"All right, Billy I'll tell you what, I also have a Jeep besides my truck. We can take it out to the mud hills and look around.

Billy shook his head yes but he still seems so sad. They left and Jay came in. I showed him the text . I explained to Jay that I didn't show Billy the text because he just looks so defeated. I thought it'd be best just to let him and Jonathan go. At that point Jay sent a mass text calling off the search until we can figure what direction to go in.

"Jay it is ok for you to get upset. I mean Cheyenne is your sister."

" Summer, I can't afford to fall apart right now. I have to keep myself together and do my job. I need to just focus on bringing my sister home."

" I know." I gave him a warm hug.

"Okay ladies the best thing you can do is go home and wait. Keep your cell phones on. Ruby Jean can take you home."

Ruby Jean and I headed out to my place. When we got there Mr. Stew and Augie were ready to eat dinner. After feeding them I sat on the couch with Ruby Jean. Augie came up to us. Ruby Jean started rubbing his ears. We talked about everything that was going on while we sat and waited.

9

Cheyenne woke up on a bed to find herself locked in a room she did not recognize. She saw a window. She got up and took a look. Cheyenne noticed she was on a second floor. Nothing looked familiar but it was dark out. Because of a light that sat in front of the house and the porch light, she was able to see that she was surrounded by the forest. The door opened and a man in a black ski mask wearing all black came in.

"Get on the bed," he demanded while holding a gun.

Cheyenne was shaking and did what he said. The killer placed sticky paper over the window so Cheyenne could not see out the window. A little bit of the outside lights still broke through. The killer stepped in the hall and then came back in. He handed her a tray with a sandwich and chips on it with a glass of milk.

"Eat!" He demanded.

Cheyenne started to cry while taking a few bites of her sandwich. The stranger went out the door and slammed his shut. She could hear him locking the door with a little click.

"Her snotty little tears won't phase me!" Hey ran down the steps and flopped on the sofa.

Pulling out his victims list from his pocket.

"I will save Cheyenne for last so the rest of them will suffer not knowing where she's at."

He took a deep sigh.

"Ok, it's time for someone to die. Next on my list you are up." Then he did an evil chuckle.

The killer sent this mass text to everyone. "Listen up, it's time for someone to fly high; but not before they die!"

"Do not engage!" Jay demanded.

The killer just chuckled.

Ruby Jean was now at Jonathan's house sitting on the sofa. She was about to fall asleep. It was midnight and it had been a long evening. Johnathan was standing in the garage with the door open. He had just lit up a cigar when he heard a loud sound then a swish went past his ear and hit the wall.

"What in the blaze was that!"

He heard another loud sound and saw a bullet shatter the right front passenger's window. He ran inside and grabbed a shotgun.

"Stay in here Ruby Jean, I mean it!"

"What, why! What's going on?

She went into Jonathan's bedroom and tried crawling under the bed. She was able to get under there from waist up and got stuck. She couldn't move so the bottom half of her was sticking out.

Jonathan went out the back door where his German Shepherd Dozer was standing at the door.

"Go on in Dozer. Go find Ruby Jean."

Jonathan slowly moved to the side of the house. He was not afraid of anything since he was an excellent shooter from hunting. He once had wrestled with alligators at the alligator park; he did two shows a day until the state shut the park down. Jonathan didn't fear anything.

"Hey, come on out you coward. I ain't afraid of you!"

Another shot went over his head. Most people would run away from gunfire but not Jonathan. He ran straight towards it. This led him into the woods across the street because a man in a black mask dressed all in black carrying a gun was running into the woods. Jonathan ran after him.

After 5 minutes he lost track of the guy.

The killer got angry with himself, he thought at least one of his shots would kill Jonathan.

When Jonathan went back in the house he yelled for Ruby

Jean. Dozer barked from the bedroom. When he walked in he saw Ruby Jean's bottom half under the bed sticking out.

"Ruby June baby, you okay?"

She didn't answer him. Hey leaned in closer and could hear her snoring.

He thought to himself, " really she fell asleep at a time like this!"

Jonathan yells ,"Ruby Jean, you can come out now!"

Her legs bounced up and down.

"What!" she said. Then she hit her head on the bed.

"Ouch!"

"Come out woman."

"Jonathan, I can't, I'm stuck!"

"Only You Ruby Jean. He shakes his head.

"Ok let me lift the bed."

He lifted the bed and she crawled out.

"Great, now I have a headache. "she scrunched her lips together.

"You'll be fine! Tomorrow I'm going to go to the police station and talk to Jay."

"I will go with you tomorrow because I need to update on Cheyenne. What happened to you when you were outside?"

"That creep came after me. I turned things on him and chased him into the woods for about 5 minutes until I lost him."

"Are you sure it was a man?"

"I'm positive, that person was way too tall to be a woman! They even ran like a man."

10

When the killer got back to the house he was furious.

"How can I let that punk get the best of me? He is going to

stay on my victims list. Now everyone will be punished!" He sent a mass text again.

"Jonathan, you have angered me. Now everyone will feel my anger tonight. You have sealed Cheyenne's fate. you will never see her again!"

"Please man, don't hurt her, she's innocent!" Billy pleaded.

"Please don't hurt her, she hasn't done anything wrong." I texted.

"Do not engage, anyone!" - Jay

Jay was out laying on my sofa for the night and I came out of my room.

"Jay I'm so scared he's going to kill Cheyenne!"

Jay took a deep breath.

"Summer, I'm scared of that too but I can't let the fear get the best of me or I'll interfere with my job. Right now my job is to bring Cheyenne home safe and alive. I don't want anyone engaging with this killer because that gives him more control and power. Tomorrow morning I'm going to go talk to Jonathan to find out what is going on."

I went back to my room to crawl back into bed and fell asleep. We got up about 8:00 a.m. It's Sunday so I don't have to work. I fed Augie and Mr. Stew then got ready and so did Jay. We left and got coffee at the coffee shop. After that we went straight to Jonathan's house.

Jonathan and Ruby Jean were there. Jonathan told us about what happened. He pointed out the bullet holes in his car window.

"That lunatic shattered my truck window that's going to cost me! I had Ruby Jean stay inside while I chased him. Man, he ain't even very good at shooting guns. He shot at me three times and didn't hit me. What does that tell ya? It tells me he's a wannabe. You hear me! A loser. Get me alone in a room with him and we'll see who tries to kill who and who wins. That's all I'm saying!"

Jonathan kept mumbling under his breath, he was irate.

Ruby Jean said "Yeah I stayed inside and tried to hide. I got stuck halfway under the bed and I couldn't move."

"Ruby Jean, you must have been scared."

"Yeah I was until I fell asleep."

I looked at Jay.

"Only You Ruby Jean, only you. "Jay shook his head.

Jay took the bullet casings for evidence we headed out and went to the police station. I finally got to meet Tommy while we were there.

"Hey Tommy, can you take this bag of evidence to the lab?

The lab is in Mayville about 20 minutes from here."

"Cool I'll just use my GPS to get there no problem at all.

Jay and I sat in his office. Billy came in and sat down.

" So, do you think Cheyenne is still alive?"

"Billy, we have to think positive to get our jobs done. So I'm trying to stay in the frame of mind that she is still alive and I need to bring her home safely."

"Okay, good! We need to figure out how this creep knows all of us. I find it strange he knows your Aunt Betty. Is there anyone that we went to school with who would hold a grudge?"

"Well, Jay you were a grade higher than us. I don't think it'd be anyone that was a grade above you. Most of the kids a grade above you didn't really want anything to do with mine and Billy's class."

"That's true. You, Billy, Cheyenne and Ruby Jean were all in the same class. I remember taking you to the prom instead of Meredith. If you think about it, that is where our love story began."

"Wow dude, you remember that you're kind of a romantic guy aren't you."

"You know it buddy. Summer doesn't have a romantic bone in her body. So one of us has to be romantic. "Jay winked at me and I smiled.

Billy shook his head yes

"That dude Jesse Penrod and I never got along. He always had a thing for Cheyenne."

"You know Billy, I remember that. He's kind of rough around the edges. I wouldn't let him date my sister. But the question is, is he a killer?"

Jay rubbed his chin while he was thinking.

"I can't help but to wonder if my sister Sabrina had another man in her life that she manipulated!" I commented

"Humm, that is possible."

I was starting to get a migraine from all this. My head was just pounding like it wanted to explode.

I had to take something.

"Jay spoke up, "I also think there is a possibility that he did not hurt Cheyenne. If you think about it, he can use her to hold over our heads."

Billy shook his head in agreement and then spoke up.

"Bro, that's a good point but why did he pick Cheyenne to kidnap?"

He threw his hands up in the air in frustration.

"Well Billy it's obvious that she is the weakest one in the group. I mean think about it. She's 5'2 and petite. She's only about 100 lbs. soaking wet. She's also a very sweet person. He was able to play into all her weaknesses. We find these things adorable about her but they still would be a weakness up against a killer."

Jay paused for a moment.

"Now, imagine if he took Ruby Jean. He would be begging us to take her back. She would drive him crazy. Not to

mention she's tall and meaty, as she likes to point out."

This made all three of us laugh. I felt good to release some tension for a brief moment.

"Man you're probably right she would drive that creep crazy for sure. He would probably turn the gun on himself."

That made us laugh harder. I feel that sometimes in a crisis people do laugh at inappropriate times to release tension. This is one of those times.

"So we know Ruby Jean does not have any enemies. I think Addison's the only one that hates Summer? Does she have any man in her life that she's close to?" Billy asked.

Jay put his pointer finger up. "You know she does have a half brother through her father and they are close. His name is Jared Fritz. He is also very standoffish like Addison. It looks like we have two men that need to come in for questioning. Billy, I want you to take care of bringing them in for questioning."

Jay's assistant came in.

"Billy, Tommy's online two. He tried calling you on your cell phone."

He looked at his cell phone and saw that the ringer was turned down.

" I didn't mean to have it turned down. I'll take Tommy's call at my desk, so I can get to work."

He left and went to his desk.

"So Jay, I never knew Addison had a brother?"

"Yeah I only met him once. I wasn't too impressed with him. They act a lot alike."

"Well, you dated her!".

"Summer but I was trying to get over you."

"Oh no Jay, I drove you into Addison's arms. Wow, I'm really sorry."

"I made peace with it. The important thing is that we are back together."

My phone dinged and so did Jay's.

"Hey you losers, since Jonathan survived the next person on my list has to go! So be on your toes, it could be you.

Ha, you never know."

"Just answer me this, is Cheyenne okay. I need to know my sister is ok and alive."

"Ha-ha big bad sheriff wouldn't you like to know! Silence for now."

Jay slammed his fist on his desk. "We need to expose this creep and fast. More lives are at stake! This lunatic killed your uncle so that tells me it's not just our circle of friends that they are after.

11

Billy was looking through a file on his computer when we were about to leave.

"Hey Jay, come take a look at this."

Jay took a good look at Billy's screen. Jesse Penrod had served time for violence and kidnapping. He just got out 6 months ago.

"Wow, that is definitely a red flag. Bring him in for

questioning and also Jared Fritz as soon as possible."

"Yeah definitely. Did you and Summer get that text just a few minutes ago? We should be trying to find out who's

next on his list. If that's even possible."

"Well Billy I do know one thing, he is not just after our circle of friends. After all, he did go after Summer's uncle."

After Jay dropped me off I loved Augie and Mr. Stew for a while. Then I called Ruby Jean and asked her to meet me at the coffee shop. These days I feel a little bit better about leaving Augie and Mr. Stew home for a while because I have an alarm with cameras thanks to Jay. I left and arrived at the coffee shop. I went in and got both of us a coffee.

"I'm back." I said to the cashier Thelma. This was my second trip here today.

"Well honey, you just come on back anytime."

I took a seat at our favorite round table. Then I saw Ruby Jean pull up. She got out of her car. She started to walk towards the coffee shop and stumbled. Her ponytail was all over the place and then fell to the back of her shirt collar. I spit out a little bit of my coffee. I tried hard not to laugh. Ruby Jean tried to play it off by walking like a model on the runway. That made me take a deep breath because my emotions were everywhere and I didn't want to burst out laughing at her.. A man at the table to the left was laughing pretty hard.

Ruby Jean came in the doors and sat down at the table, her fake ponytail is just dangling barely and holding on to the back of her collar.

A little boy with his mother yelled "look Mommy the big lady has her hamster with her, can I pet it?"

"Caleb, that is not a hamster. Now be quiet!"

I was trying so hard not to laugh again. The man at the table couldn't stop laughing.

I got up and stood behind Ruby Jean and fixed her ponytail. Then gave her a hug from behind.

"I love you Ruby Jean, don't ever change."

Ruby Jean had a confused look on her face. "Ok I won't ." I sat back down.

"Summer, it's just weird not having Cheyenne sitting here with us!"

I felt angry and sad again. "I know!"

Cheyenne, who was well and alive, decided to crawl through the vent. It took her a while to pull the vent cover off. She was able to crawl through to the main room downstairs. Then she kicked the vent cover off and climbed out. She knew the killer left while it was still dark out and didn't come back for a long time. She decided she still had to hurry so she dashed for the front door to unlock it and open it. She ran through it while her heart beat faster and faster. Cheyenne did not take the main trail down where his car would come through. She didn't want to get caught so she ran into the woods.

When Cheyenne felt like she was far enough away she started walking. She walked for a few hours before she ended up running into a main road and found a gas station. She walked in and walked to the counter where a cashier was standing. She then begged the cashier to use his phone.

"Sir, can I use your phone? I've been kidnapped. My brother is a sheriff and I need him to come get me."

" Oh wow, yes no problem!"

Cheyenne called Jay. "Please come get me!"

"Cheyenne, we all have been so worried, where are you? Are you okay?"

"I'm ok, let me find out where I'm at."

"Sir where am I at, please?"

"Ma'am you're in Alabama. You're about an hour from the

Alabama Mississippi line."

"Oh I'm from Mississippi, Blue Ash Mississippi."

"All right, we'll see, from Mississippi cross over the state line and then you drive about an hour and we'll be here on the right hand side. You're standing in the Gas and Go Mart. We are the only gas station that you will see. Any

another gas station is about 15 miles from here."

"Jay, did you get all that?"

"I did and I'm on my way. It'll take me a little while to get

there. So just hang tight!"

Cheyenne went back outside after thanking the man. She paced back and forth and her nerves were on edge. Jay finally arrived with Billy. They both got out of the car and gave her a warm hug. They headed back to Jay's house. Jay didn't push Cheyenne to talk about what happened. He figured you'd talk about it when she was ready. She took a nap and slept for a long time.

Ruby Jean and myself went to Jay's house and sat on the couch. Jonathan headed over. Tommy stopped by as well to be supportive. When Cheyenne woke up from her nap everyone was sitting down in the front room. Everyone got up and gave

Cheyenne a group hug.

"Little lady, we were so scared. He threatened to kill you. Then he would not say if he did!" Billy was getting choked up and put his fists to his mouth.

"Cheyenne I am so thankful you are okay we were very worried" I said.

"I don't even know you and I was worried and missed you. Tommy commented it made us laugh.

Jonathan came through the door. "All right whose butt do

I need to kick?" we all laughed again.

"Well the killer had a black mask and dressed in all black the whole time. I know I was on the second floor in a house surrounded by forest. I only got to look out the window briefly once. He came in and covered it with black sticky paper. Sunlight still shone through so I could tell he left when it was still dark out and came back after it had been dark out for a while. He never tried to hurt me. He just barked orders."

"One thing we do know for sure is that you were in Alabama!"

So a house in the forest could be anywhere. There are also several houses in the forest from here to there.

"Little lady come here." She went over and sat on Billy's lap and he gave her a warm long hug. He was so happy to have her back.

"Now we have to worry about who this maniac will go after next or if he will try to snatch me again!" Cheyenne's voice was shaky.

"Please everyone, I can't stress enough, be aware of your surroundings. Do not engage with this crazy person when he sends texts. That is just fueling his fire." Jay's was stern.

Everyone left so that Cheyenne could get more rest. I decided to pull over and get more gas since I was running low. The guy at the pump behind me was giving me the creeps. A chill ran down my spine. He stared at me and glared . He never took his eyes off of me. I finished up, paid at the pump and took off very quickly.

I got out of my car and started to walk towards my condo. Then I froze. Another chill ran down my spine. A man dressed in all black with a ski mask on was standing in front of the building. He held his gun out towards me. I quickly grabbed my gun out of my purse. He fired a shot that went past me. I fired back at him and grazed his left shoulder. My next door neighbor came out to see what was going on. That's when the man in black took off running in the direction of a neighborhood that sat to the left. He disappeared into the night.

"Summer are you okay? Did that creep shoot at you?"

"He did Mr. Baker, I'm okay."

"My wife called the cops."

Jay pulled up into the parking lot. Glenn pulled up right behind him.

"Glenn told me and I heard your address on the scanner. Are you ok Summer?" Jay gave me a warm hug.

"I am Jay, I'm just a little shaken. I believe that was the killer who was dressed in black with a black ski mask. He shot at me. I shot at him back and I think I nicked his shoulder. Also there was a creepy guy at the gas station that kept staring and glaring at me the whole time. Do you think they are connected?"

"Oh man, I'm sorry Summer. There's a good possibility they might be connected. It just seems kind of odd that this man in black would be here right after you were at the gas station. So they really could be connected." Billy said while shaking his head.

Jay made a long sigh. " Okay Summer, let's get you upstairs and inside to safety."

I thank Mr. Baker. He nodded his head at me.

" Boss man, you want me to write up a report on this and put it on your desk."

"That'd be great Glen. Also maybe you could give Billy a ride back to the station."

We got greeted by Augie when we came inside my condo. I fed them a snack and then sat down next to Jay on the couch.

" I really think maybe you should stay at my place tonight."

"Jay you know I can't leave Augie and Mr. Stew alone overnight with all this craziness going on. I will be fine, go home and take care of your sister. I have cameras and an alarm system now thanks to you. So I'm good! But thank

you for loving me!"

Truth is, I was still a little shaken up. I'm just not going to let this psycho run me out of my own place.

"Ok, after I leave please double check everything. I will have a patrol car drive by often throughout the night."

When my alarm goes off a notification goes straight to my phone and Jay's phone. Jay headed out and I headed to bed. I laid in bed and stared at the ceiling until I fell asleep.

12

I was exhausted when I got up. I went ahead and fed Mr. Stew and Augie.

"Mr. Stew thought to himself, "Finally some fish in my food!"

Mr. Stew made "num-num- num" noises as he ate.

I laughed. " I guess you like your new food Mr. Stew!"

I told Jay I was going into work because I wanted to keep things more normal. Plus I will need to be off tomorrow for my uncle's funeral. I get ready for work and go on in.

The first people I see when I walk in are Bailey and the other new girl Lisa.

Then Ruby Jean came up from the back.

" Summer, look I shined up my ring! Ain't it purity?" Ruby Jean gave me a big toothy smile.

"Ruby Jean is really beautiful."

Ruby Jean started to swing her hips and arms while singing.

"I'm getting married la la la la. Oh yeah oh yeah I'm getting married! you are not!

She looks straight at Addison who walked up from the back.

"Ruby Jean, maybe you should be singing that to Summer. I mean shouldn't summer be married by now? She folded her arms across her chest tilting her head and looked at me.

" Well Addison, I'm not in a hurry to get married because I already have him." I looked back at her and smirked.

"Alright Addison it's time for you to leave since you're not working."

Addison rolled her eyes at me and walked to the back to leave.

" Lisa, I'm the store manager Summer."

"Hi. Thanks for hiring me. The guy Wyatt that interviewed me was a nice guy."

"Yeah he's the owner's husband. He's in here quite often."

"Wyatt said that you're a really good manager and you're pretty cool."

"Well that was nice of Wyatt." I smiled.

Bailey cleared her throat and sighed while rolling her eyes.

I let it go because Bailey was being petty like Addison always does. Seems like Addison has started to rub off onto her. Two haircuts came in and they were regular clients.

"Joe, Bailey would be happy to take you back and cut your hair." She went ahead and took him back with a smile on her face.

"Jenny, Lisa would be glad to cut your hair."

" I sure will. Come back to my station."

My client came in a few minutes later and I had her take a seat.

"Hey Emma, how are you?"

"I'm excited to get my highlights. Can you give me the wolf card also?"

" I sure can that would look great on you!" She gave me a big smile.

" I will be right back, I'm going to get everything set up."

I gave her a few magazines to look at. I came back up with my rolling cart that has everything laid out on it. I looked over at Bailey and I saw Ruby Jean standing behind Joe with clippers.

I thought to myself "Not again!"

I walked over to them. "What's going on over here? Is everything ok?"

Bailey just stood there with her arms crossed over her chest rolling her eyes with a sour look on her face.

"Well, Bailey made a boo-boo." Ruby Jean answered.

I looked closer at Joe's head and saw a hole in his hair that went down to the scalp.

"Joe, I'm so sorry. You don't have to pay today and I'll give you a few free haircuts."

"I appreciate that Summer, but is it that bad?"

"Unfortunately Joe you can see a bald spot in your hair so the only way to fix it is for Ruby Jean to take it down to a skin fade."

"Wow, that is short! I usually get a four guard. What happened?"

"I'm sorry I forgot to put the guard on my clippers." Bailey uttered.

"If you would have started from the bottom this might be a little more fixable." I snapped.

"Well Summer, I have never done a clipper cut before I'm just out of school!" "Don't say another word, we will talk about this, now go to the back."

Bailey stomped to the back and sat at the table. I got done placing foils in Emma's hair. Addison was sitting with her and the back door was left open.

Addison spoke up." Is there some reason you always pick on Bailey?"

"I don't pick on her. She has messed up three heads and cost this shop a lot of money!"

This is when Wyatt came in through the back door.

"Ok ladies I heard some of this conversation. First of all Summer doesn't pick on anyone, she's a great manager. Second Bailey, I should have had you do a haircut for me before hiring you. Summer is right, you're making our shop lose a lot of money by giving away services to make up for your bad service!"

"I have never done a clipper cut, they didn't teach me that in school!"

"Bailey, you should have asked for help!" I commented

"She is teachable, you don't want to teach her."

"Well Addison, Bailey clearly is not ready for the floor and this is not a teaching salon. So if Summer doesn't fire you then I will." Wyatt got mad.

" Thank you Wyatt for having my back."

"Girl I always have your back, you know I like you."

Wyatt spoke up again "Go home Addison you're not even on the clock."

" I'm calling my mom Wyatt !"

"You go right ahead Addison and call your mommy; because your mother has been telling you for years to grow up and stop acting like a spoiled brat." Addison stomped through the back door.

"Bailey I disagree with Addison, You're not teachable because of your attitude. As long as you carry that then you will never be teachable. Go ahead, pack your stuff and get out!" Wyatt added.

She went to her station and started to pack.

"I have always wanted to say that to someone !" Wyatt chuckled.

"That doesn't surprise me Wyatt."

All of a sudden we heard a crash that came from the cutting floor. We hurried up there to see Bailey had slammed the glass product shelves to the ground. It was a heaping mess with shattered glass everywhere. Bailey then went to the lobby and grabbed one of the chairs. She threw it at the mirror for my station.

The glass shattered everywhere.

"What has this demon child done?" Wyatt says with a disgusted look on his face.

We had two male clients in the shop at the time and they both made Bailey sit down in a chair. Wyatt told the two customers that helped out that they have two free haircuts coming to them for their help.

I called Jay and he was here in about 20 minutes with Tommy.

"That looks like a tornado hit it." Tommy commented.

Ruby jeans spoke up "I guess we won't be selling any of these products. You are going to have to pay for your little tantrum. You know I never did like you Addison number two. You have no manners! Shameful!"

Jay made Bailey clean up the whole mess by herself, which took two hours.

I commented, "She's buddies with Addison." Jay shook his head and chuckled.

He handcuffed Bailey as she yelled at me, "This is not over! Watch your back, Summer!"

That irritated Jay so he handcuffed her tighter.

"Hey that hurts!"

"Good!" he replied. And they left.

Emma's hair turned out beautiful. The rest of the evening at the shop was pretty peaceful. We finished the closing duties at the shop and headed to our cars. Wyatt reached his car parked in the front while Ruby Jean and I were parked on the left side. Ruby Jean and I were still talking when we heard a popping sound then I felt a sting in my left side. I dropped to the ground and passed out.

I woke up the next morning in the hospital. Jay was sitting in a chair next to my hospital bed. He had his eyes closed.

"Jay!"

My left side just had a sharp sting. " Ouch ,wow! What happened?

" You were shot last night, Summer, try not to move. I have got to catch this guy you almost died!"

"Will you hand me my phone Jay, Please?"

He grabbed my phone from the counter or where my clothes were sitting. I had a new text come in from the killer.

"So I hear you got shot. I saw it in the news. Too bad I can't take credit for it. Kudos to the one that shot you."

"Jay the psycho claims he did not shoot me!"

Jay paused for a moment and rubbed his chin like he always does when he's contemplating.

"Huh, Addison bailed Bailey out."

"With Daddy's money no doubt!" I mumbled.

He shook his head. I will have Bailey brought in for questioning."

"One thing is for sure. That person who shot me was a better shot than the killer." Jay shook his head in agreement. Then he called Tommy to bring Bailey in for questioning.

"Jay, I need to go home and take care of Augie and Mr. Stew."

"My love, you need to slow down. You were just shot. You need to rest! Besides Ruby Jean and Jonathan are checking on them frequently. Cheyenne is resting up just a little bit more so she can go back to work."

I text Ruby Jean about Mr. Stew and Augie. She and Jonathan were heading over there right now to feed them. When they arrived they were greeted by Augie. They sat on the couch for a minute to love Augie.

"Hey boy how are you?" Jonathan scratches behind Augie's ears.

Mr. Stew was on his post crouched down glaring at them.

"Well, I guess I should feed them now."

Ruby Jean got up and went into the kitchen to get their food ready.

"You're looking really friendly over there Mr. Stew."

Jonathan went over to try to pet Mr. Stew and got swatted at.

"Now see, this is why I'm a dog person. Me and cats just don't mix. I don't understand them and they don't understand me!"

" Mr. Stew thought to himself," That's right big boy, back off and don't touch me!" Augie finished his food, so Jonathan took him out to use the bathroom.

"If I bring your bowl over to you, are you going to eat me? I mean you did try to eat my ponytail! before?"

Mr. Stew just glared at Ruby Jean while she set his food down.

Ruby Jean took one finger to slowly pet Mr Stew on the head. Mr. Stew started to purr. She then took her whole hand and continued to pet him while he was purring. She ran her finger down his back to his tail. When she touched his tail he hissed and bit her.

"Ouch you little demon that hurts!"

When Jonathan came back in he saw Ruby Jean running her hand underwater.

"That little demon bit me!"

"Well women, did you have enough sense not to try to pet him? You know he's not friendly. You saw him trying to swat at me. Let's just get out of here. We can check on them again tonight or have Jay do it."

OVER AT CHEYENNE PLACE Jay put cameras and an alarm system in for her . He also helped her get a trained German Shepherd named Jack. She was lying on the sofa with Jack when she got a text. "Enjoy your freedom for now!"

She sent that text to Jay.

He replied. "got it!"

Hearing from the killer gave her chills down her spine and made her heart race. She shut her eyes and tried to relax.

13

I wasn't released from the hospital until Thursday morning. This meant I missed my uncle's funeral. My Aunt Betty did visit me in the hospital along with Ruby Jean, Jonathan, Cheyenne and Billy. Not all at once though.

When I got home Mr. Stew and Augie were thrilled to see me. I sat on the sofa and they both came over to get loved on. Jay had to leave and go back to the station because they located Bailey, finally. I decided to take a nap. Unfortunately the break from the killer was short-lived.

"Wake up, no more rest, someone has to die!"-Unknown

I thought to myself, "Here we go again!"

"Ha, ha you idiot you can't even shoot a gun correctly. You have missed every time!" -Jonathan

"Laugh now, but maybe next time I won't miss."-Unknown

"How many times do I have to say this, do not engage anyone!" -Jay

---

BAILEY WAS SITTING in one of the interrogation rooms. Jay went in and sat down across from her.

"Bailey, are you aware of why you were brought in?"

"Look I didn't shoot Summer, that's ridiculous! I don't even know how to shoot a gun. You should be talking to Addison. Aren't you the one who taught her how to shoot a gun? Besides I wasn't even in town I was in Mayville at my dad's house. You can check with him or my stepmother."

Jay got quiet for a moment rubbing his chin.

"So tell me why do you think it was Addison?"

"Like I said Jay you are the one that taught how to shoot a gun. I've been hanging out with her and I've heard all about the past. She is definitely not over you. She still hates Summer and wishes she was dead. I'm not trying to throw her under the bus because she is my friend but I just won't take the rap for her. I know my anger got the best of me when I was in the shop and I am sorry for that. I was raised better than that."

Jay could feel his jaw tightening up and his blood pressure climbing.

"Okay Bailey, if your alibi checks out then you're free to go." Jim left the room called down the hall to Billy.

"Hey Billy, I need you to go get Addison with me. We need to bring her in for questioning and you know how that will go!"

Billy rolled his eyes. "Man do I!"

Jay and Billy headed out to Addison's place. They pulled up and saw her car sitting in front of her condo. They got out and knocked on her door. The door popped open so they went in.

Jay called out, "Addison are you here?"

It was silent. Her bedroom door was jarred and a light was on. Jay opened the door to see Addison on the floor. Her dresser had stuff knocked off to the ground and her mattress was turned sideways. It looked like a struggle took place.

"You've got to be kidding me!" Jay said.

Jay rolled Addison over and felt for a pulse but he knew she was gone. Her eyes are still wide open. He knelt down next to Addison, shut her eyes and prayed over her. Jay and Billy started to look around. When Jay looked in her nightstand he saw her gun laying there in the drawer. He put on gloves and unloaded the gun so it could be placed in a bag for evidence. If she did shoot Summer, having a murder weapon is a big deal.

30 minutes later Nancy the coroner's office pulled up and came in.

"Hey Nancy. Billy, you remember Nancy from the coroner's office." He nodded at her and smiled.

"Jay, is this Addison your ex-girlfriend?"

"She is and I'm just as shocked."

"Wow Jay I'm sorry." She knelt next to Addison.

"If I had to call it right now I would say this is a strangulation. I still need to do a full autopsy."

"Thanks Nancy I guess I won't get answers just yet but I do suspect her of shooting Summer."

"Well is Summer ok? This is starting to seem like a love triangle gone bad." "Summer is going to be ok, she's just recovering right now. Can you check for a gun residue on Addison's hands and fingernails."

"Absolutely Jay!"

"Great, thanks Nancy."

LATER JAY STOPPED BY my place. We sat on the sofa.

"So I don't believe the killer shot you, I believe he was telling the truth about that. Bailey's alibi checked out, but she did tell me I should be speaking to Addison and she thinks Addison shot you."

"What Addison hates me so much that she would shoot me. Well then you need to arrest her right away!"

I felt my blood pressure rising in my face as it became hot."

"Well here's the thing, Addison was murdered!" I cannot believe my ears!

"Wait a minute, what did you just say Addison was murdered. Are you kidding me? But who, why, how!"

"We're still working on the details but it looks like a strangulation." I shook my head in disgust.

"Now a lab will be able to tell us for sure if she was the one that shot you."

A group text came through from unknown

"I took care of that Addison for all you losers. You should be thanking me."

" Really, Addison's dead?" Ruby Jean text

"She is, stop engaging." Jay text

I looked at Jay. " Jay this is crazy, what reason would they have to kill her?"

" Summer, she was probably on their hit list already. I have to head back to the station. Double check everything after I leave. Love you!"

"I love you too!"

Jay headed out. I double checked everything then laid down for a while.

I wanted to call Beverly but I wasn't sure she knew yet.

14

Two days later I met Cheyenne and Ruby Jean at the coffee shop. This has been a ritual for us for the last couple of years. The owner Cynthia is a lovely woman.

"Hi ladies, would you care for a pastry on the house?"

We all thanked her and picked out a pastry. Then she came back over to talk.

I saw in the news last night Addison Bell was murdered? How awful. I do know her mother Beverly. We went to school together. She was always such a kind person. I can't imagine what she's going through. Addison must have gotten her mean streak from her father.

I spoke up. "I really do feel bad for Beverly, she is a very nice lady."

" Were you ladies friends with Addison outside the shop" "Ooh, gosh no. She was a snot!" Ruby Jean blurted.

" Well, Ruby Jean, don't hold back on how you feel!" Cynthia smirked.

"Will you ladies be going to the funeral?"

"Yes, we will be there to support Beverly." I said while looking at Ruby Jean and Cheyenne.

"Well good, I will see you all at the funeral on Saturday." Beverly decided to shut the shop down for a week.

We were drinking our coffee in silence for a moment when my phone rang. It was Wyatt.

"Hey Wyatt, how is Beverly doing?"

"She's been doing a lot of crying but she is holding up."

"Oh, Wyatt, I'm sorry. I hope you're okay?"

"I'm okay, I just want to be here for my wife. Let me tell you why I called. Beverly wants to sell the shop to you. So can you come to the shop so we can talk?"

"Wow, okay I can be there in 10 minutes."

"Great, see you then."

"Well ladies I'm heading to the shop Beverly wants to talk about a few things with me."

They both smiled and nodded. I headed out and reached the shop. I saw Beverly's car. She and Wyatt live in

Maysville, so they live pretty close.

I headed in and they were sitting at the break room table. Beverly looked tired and like she had been wiping her eyes from crying.

"Hello Summer, please come take a seat." Beverly smiled at me.

I thought back for a moment when we all thought Beverly was going to be like Addison and she's just the opposite.

Wyatt put a chair out for me and I took a seat.

"Summer as you know from what Wyatt told you on the phone I want to sell my salon to you. My sister who was such a sweet woman; my daughter who wasn't very kind, were both connected to the shop. Currently it just gives me painful memories.

"I know this shop is worth a lot more but I want to sell it to you for $20,000. The shop is really your baby, you're the one who has worked so hard to keep it going and running. You have been here for several years now. Wyatt told me

how much you care for the shop and the clients."

"Gosh Beverly I don't know what to say!"

"Say yes summer, and relieve me of this burden. The shop

right now is just a thorn that keeps poking me."

Okay, I will buy it if Wyatt stays on as my manager."

Heck yeah girl you know I will! I love this place too."

"WELL THAT'S VERY GENEROUS of you Summer because Wyatt does love this place.

Wonderful Summer, I will have my lawyer draw up paperwork for you to sign. Will you be paying the whole thing

up front or will you be making payments? "

"I still have money from my father's company when it was sold. I also still have money for when both my parents

passed away. I can pay the whole amount."

"Oh good, we can do this Tuesday at my lawyer's office. I hope you can make it to Addison's funeral. I know you two had your differences."

"Unfortunately Beverly she might be the one that shot me."

Beverly started to cry. "Summer, I am so sorry I know Addison needed help, but she refused to get it. Since she was a grown woman I couldn't make her do anything."

"Beverly ,this is not your fault!"

"I will be there to support you and Wyatt."

I hugged her and said goodbye and left.

I reached my condo and before I got out my phone dinged.

"Hey Queen bee, I hope you and your workers you call friends will be at the funeral on Saturday?" -Unknown

"How do you know that psycho?"

"Summer I'm everywhere and I know everything!"

"That's impossible just stay away you creep!"

He never responded back. So I got out of my car and went up the stairs. I can hear Augie sniffing on the other side of the door. I opened the door and he was wagging his tail and prancing around.

"Come sit on the sofa with me."

I sat down and he jumped up next to me. Mr. Stew was on his post glaring at us.

"Mr. Stew, stop being grumpy and come sit next to me." He jumped down and jumped up next to me. I started to pet him.

15

Saturday afternoon we all were at the funeral but not many people came. How sad is that. Beverly was sitting with Wyatt tears streaming down her face and Wyatt was trying to comfort her. Addison's father was on the other side with his wife. He looked a bit stressed. Addison's brother was sitting behind them. He looked very upset.

Jay and I got up to go over and give Beverly a hug.

"Hello Jay, it's been awhile. I always wanted to apologize for Addison's obsession with you. My daughter definitely had problems.

"Beverly, don't even worry about it, it's fine. I just hate that you're going through this right now. If you need anything let me know. Wyatt, are you good?"

"I'm holding up, thanks man!"

We sat back down. It was kind of a lonely and sad feeling when I looked around again and saw that there really aren't a lot of people. I thought for sure some more people would come through the door. It's just a few family members and a few clients and of course our group. Addison couldn't seem to get along with most people. Most of her clients tolerated her because she was really good at what she did. I looked at the doors one more time and spotted Bailey sitting in the back. She looks sad and lonely. My heart went out to her.

"Jay, I'm going to call Bailey over to sit with us. She looks so sad."

"My love you have such a good heart!"

I looked back at Bailey and waved her on to come sit next to me. She got up and came over. As soon as she sat down she burst into tears and I comforted her.

"Summer I'm sorry!"

I placed a piece of her hair behind her ear.
    "It's okay Bailey, we can talk about this after the funeral."
When the funeral was over we all headed to the grave site and we started to walk over from our cars only to see a stand with black roses on it.
    "Seriously, again!" Billy blurted out.
    "Jay, please tell me you will catch this sicko!" Beverly's voice shook.
    "Yes ma'am, I'm still working on the case."
After the burial we all decided to go to lunch.

I invited Bailey to go with us. We were all munching on appetizers when Bailey spoke up. "I am sorry for my behavior on the last day at the shop . I have no excuse for trashing the shop!" Everyone shook their heads yes.

" Summer I want to come back to the shop.I will do anything!" I took a deep breath and spoke.

"Here's what I can do. I can bring you back on as a receptionist for 90 days. During that time Wyatt and I will train you for everything. Also the rest of the people here that work in the shop will train you. When Wyatt and I aren't working and you are working I will assign you to someone for your shift that you can shadow and learn from. Our clients have always had top notch service and I don't want that to change. Every single stylist in the shop has amazing skills so we just need to get you there. That included people skills. I know it took a lot for you to apologize and ask for a job back."

"Oh good thank you Summer, thank you so much!

Will Beverly be okay with me coming back?"

" Well about that I do have some news for everyone. Beverly is selling the shop to me and I'm renaming it. Actually this will take place on Tuesday at Beverly's lawyers office.

" Well sweet graham crackers, that is awesome!" Ruby Jean clapped her hands together."

" Well finally some good news for a change.

"Is Wyatt going to stay on?"

"Yes, he's going to stay as the manager."

"Sweet, what are you going to name the shop?"

" The new name is Summer Styles." "Cool." Billy commented.

"I love it!" Ruby Jean clapped her hands again with a toothy smile.

A group text came in.

" I hope you'll enjoy the black roses. Ha-ha!" -Unknown

" Do not engage!" Jay demanded .

Beau walked in and sat down.

"Yes, I'm late. I don't have to explain myself to anyone. Now where is the waitress?" I chuckled to myself, typical Beau .

"Hmmm, I'm surprised to see you here Bailey." Beau was being sarcastic.

"Bailey's coming back to work at the shop and we are going to train her the correct way. By the way I'm buying the shop and it's happening on Tuesday. And we will be opening a week from Tuesday."

"Okay, well look at you go girl." Beau smirked at me.

"Thanks, and Wyatt will be staying on as manager."

"Why didn't Wyatt just keep the shop?"

"He loves the shop but he is considering Beverly's feelings first."

"She no longer wants to be financially tied to the shop because it is a reminder of her sister and Addison."

"I see, can't blame her there. Wyatt and I are buddies so it's pretty cool he's staying on."

"Yeah he's a great manager and I'm so thankful to have everyone stay onboard with me. I talked to Lisa and she's going to stay also. Now I was wondering what y'all think, you can either be paid hourly or by commission. Everyone has to do the same thing though. Unless you are just coming into the shop as a new employee of course that would be hourly. The commission would be 60/40. You would make 60% and I'm not going to charge booth rental. We already have a lot of clientele established and it keeps growing so you all should make pretty good money.

Everyone is responsible for their own tools and hair products. I will supply the rest."

Everyone shook their heads in agreement and I saw a lot of smiles at the table. "Well this will be way better because Beverly wanted 50% and charged a booth rental.

"Yep true but I want you all to make money. Beverly is a very sweet lady but she's just not good business wise and I think she knows that. Okay now remember we'll be opening a week from Tuesday. I will slowly be making renovations because it's expensive. I can't wait to open the shop again. Thanks everyone!"

16

Tuesday afternoon and I brought Jay with me to Beverly's lawyer's office. His secretary let us into a conference room where Beverly and Wyatt were already seated.

"Hello." I said.

We sat down across from them.

Beverly gave me a warm smile and so did Wyatt. "Wyatt, we will have to sit and figure everything out? Beverly I hope you don't mind that I'm changing the name to Summer Cuts?"

"Oh Summer, feel free, that's a cute name!" Beverly winked at me.

"I like it too!" Wyatt smiled.

Mr. Roberts entered the room.

"Hello, I'm Mr. Roberts Beverly's lawyer." He shook hands with Jay and I.

Jay smiled at everyone and remained quiet.

I handed the cashier's check to Mr Roberts. He took me through the paperwork to sign and explained everything.

"Okay great now I will have my secretary notarize everything and make copies so I will be right back."

"Oh goodness what a weight off my back thank you again for buying my shop Summer." Beverly teared up. Wyatt hugged her and handed her some tissues.

"Beverly please feel free to come in whenever you need your hair done and I will do it for no charge whenever you come in."

"Thank you so much I might just take you up on that offer someday. Maybe it'll help me to see some positives in the shop."

Mr. Roberts came back in with copies he handed to Beverly and copies he handed to myself. He also handed me back my check.

I felt confused. "I don't understand?"

"I want you to keep it. Let it go towards whatever changes you want to make to your salon." Beverly said.

"Beverly I don't know what to say thank you so much you've been very kind to me." " You're welcome Summer. I've always seen you as a good, decent lady. Now I will get out of here because I know you have things to go over. Thanks again Summer." Jay stayed quiet sitting next to me while Wyatt and I went over everything. I was so thankful he came with me. Wyatt went ahead and sent a text to everyone to meet at the shop tonight at 5:00 p.m. for a shop meeting. After we all left the lawyers office Jay took me to lunch. We talked about changes I wanted to make to the shop. "If you tell me what colors you want, I will get you a new sign and install it. I'm going to guess you want pink." "You know me so well Jay" I chuckled.

"You know someday I want to have a pink house."

"You hate the thought of that don't you?" Jay paused then chuckled.

"I guess if it's tastefully done it would be okay."

We finished eating then Jay dropped me off at my place. I played with Augie and Mr. Stew a little.

I could hear a commotion coming from the parking lot. I looked out the window. Two police cruisers pulled up in front of my building. Then I saw a third one and it looked like Jay. I went downstairs to see what was going on.

They all went into the baker's condo so I waited outside. Jay came back out.

"Jay what's going on?"

"Unfortunately another murder. Mr Baker." I had my phone with me and it dinged.

"Your neighbor should have minded his own business!" Unknown text.

I showed the text to Jay.

"Mr. Baker was just looking out for me!" I shook my head in anger.

Billy took Mrs. Baker to his Cruise and let her sit in there. She was extremely upset and crying. I walked over to her and gave her a hug because she had the door open. I went back upstairs to check on Mr. Stew and Augie while Jay greeted Nancy the

coroner.

They both went inside and went to the bedroom and saw Mr Baker lying on the bed.

"Looks like they got him when he was sleeping," Jay pointed out.

"He probably never woke up. The thing about this killer is they are all over the place and most serial killers use the same pattern of killing with their victims. This guy has been killed in different ways. Like I said he's just all over the place.

Definitely new to killing!"

"Hey that's a good point Nancy!"

"I really do think that these are revenge killings so they're personal." Nancy commented.

"Thanks for the information Nancy."

"No problem Jay, glad to help."

IT WAS 4:45 P.M. WHEN I pulled up to the shop. Everyone except for Ruby Jean was there and sitting at the stations. I went ahead and took a seat at my station. I wanted Wyatt to lead most of the meeting since he was the store manager. It was about to start when Ruby Jean stumbled through the doors. She had her hair pulled up and quite a few bobby pins in the back. No ponytail which was unusual for her and no makeup.

Beau spoke up. "Ruby Jean girl, what is up with all those bobby pins in the back of your head?"

"What, oh." she touched the back of her head.

Ruby Jean scrunched her face up. "I forgot to put my ponytail on!"

She laughed a little as she sat down. "Looks like you forgot your face as well." She touched her face.

"Y'all just quit picking on me! Making me feel ugly!" she growled.

"All right let's get this meeting started." Wyatt asserted.

"Ok, first thing Summer is going to be our new owner. Beverly is selling to her. Summer might have some new rules that we will have to go by. The new shop name will be called Summer Styles. A new sign will be put up before we open a week from today. This place will slowly get a facelift. The chemical towels will be black and the shampoo towels will be pink. The capes will also be pink. Summer I placed the order for the towels and I hired the same accountant that my wife used for the shop. She's already familiar with the books and payroll. The new hours will be?" Wyatt looked over at me.

"I've decided the hours will be 10:00 a.m. to 8:00 p.m. Tuesday through Friday.

Saturday 9:00 to 5:00. Sunday and Monday we will be closed."

"Sweet!" Cheyenne smiled.

Wyatt went on, " You will work on commission and it will be 60/40. You buy your own supplies. Except for shampoo, conditioners, perms and hair color. In other words you will buy your own tools and hair products. Be thankful there's no booth rental. With 60% commission you should make some good money. Back to you

Summer."

"I think everyone will make plenty of money at 60% commission with no booth rental. Where are you going to find that? The shop is already busy but I'd like to see more stylists, a nail tech or two and a few tanning beds."

"This is going to be awesome," Lisa spoke up.

Beau spoke up. "Wyatt man, I'm surprised you stayed on?"

"Why is that? I love the shop and Summer asked me to stay as acting manager so it works out."

"I know you love the shop but why didn't you keep it?"

"As much as I love this shop, I love my wife more. Look I didn't think I could ever love after losing Dottie yet here we are. I want to keep my wife happy and she's okay with me staying on as manager."

"Right on man, right on." Beau answered.

We finished up the meeting and went to leave. Everyone had the driver side tire flat with a smiley sticking out of it.

"Are you kidding me!" I barked.

Everyone got a text including Lisa and Bailey.

"Looks like you all had a full house at your gathering tonight. Enjoy their smiley faces complimentary from yours truly!" Unknown text.

"Okay, who is this freak that has my number? This country girl doesn't miss when she aims!"

"I'm sorry Lisa, we don't know who it is. Bailey, did you get a text as well?"

"I did Summer, How does he have our numbers? Lisa and I are brand new to the shop!"

"Well, I'm keeping my smiley face because he's cute!" said Ruby Jean.

"Oh my word, Ruby Jean. These smiley faces are not cute. They're just a warning that he knows where we're at. He's a killer now let that sink in." Lisa said

"Only You Ruby Jean, only you!" Beau chuckled.

We have someone coming out to fix everyone's tire.

JAY CAME OVER WHEN I got home. After feeding Mr Stew and Augie, I sat next to him on the sofa and told him what happened.

" Summer, Nancy thinks this guy is all over the place. His victims are killed in different ways. Usually a killer will kill all his victims the same way. They have a pattern. Since this guy is all over the place he will make a mistake." Jay and I both scrunched our faces.

"What is that smell? "Jay commented.

Augie was stretched across us with his head laying next to me.

"Augie is that you?"

He gives us a toothy smile and wags his tail.

I laugh because he's so cute when he does that.

Mr. Stew was sitting on the back of the sofa and he reached down with his paw and slapped Augie in the face twice. Then he got down from the sofa and jumped on his cat post.

Mr. Stew thought to himself, "That is disgusting. Stupid fur ball, he is not cute!"

"Augie, I think you offended Mr. Stew!"

Augie gave another toothy smile and wagged his tail. Jay chuckled.

"I'll take him out for a bathroom break."

When they were gone. I talked to Mr. Stew.

"Mr. Stew, why are you so mean to Augie? He's such a sweet boy."

Mr. Stew thought to himself, "That fur ball is more like an itch that won't go away!"

"Mr. Stew you're a grouchy old man but I love you."

I turned and looked at Mr. Stew and he was snoring away. I chuckled.

Jay came back in with Augie.

"So anyways that psycho flatten everyone's tire tonight with the stick pen that had a smiley on the end."

"Sounds familiar! This guy is definitely an amateur. I will need all those stick pins for evidence. Tell everyone to save theirs."

Jay left and I sent everyone a mass text telling everyone to save their stick pen for evidence.

RUBY JEAN WAS SITTING with Jonathan watching TV when she looked at her phone.

"Oh, boo!"

"What's wrong muffin?"

"The killer stuck smiley stick pins and everybody's tires. Summer says we must give them to her for Jay to put in evidence. I want to keep mine, it's cute!

Jonathan threw his hands in the air and his head back."Woman, what in tarnation are you thinking?

He's a killer Ruby Jean! There ain't nothing cute about anything he does!"

"But it's so cute!"

Ruby Jean I don't care if it's c-u-t-e! Jonathan said sarcastically.

"Fine !" Ruby Jean pushed her bottom lip out and crossed her arms over her chest.

Another group text came through.

"Does anyone want to meet for coffee at 9:00 tomorrow ?" Cheyenne text.

We all answered yes except Bailey. "I'm sorry maybe next time."

THE NEXT MORNING WE all met and got a bigger table. Lisa started to open up about her life.

"So Lisa, where are you from?" I smiled.

"Georgia, a small town called Peaks. My mama lives there. My daddy lives here with his wife and my sister Casey."

"Is that what brought you here, family? "Cheyenne asked.

"Somewhat, I was engaged to a cheater!" Everyone got quiet.

"Ladies it's okay, I'm not even sure I wanted to marry him. Trust me I'm doing just fine by myself. You can't keep a good woman down. I'm happy and if the right man comes along I will know it. This time I am leaning on God to guide me."

"You seem independent and strong. I admire that." I commented.

Lisa smiled. She is a tall beautiful brunette with hazel eyes and hair down her back. I love her thick Georgia accent. She's a feisty woman. I can tell she's going to fit in just fine with us.

"So do you ladies like to read?" We all answered yes.

"Cool, I do as well. We should have a book night at my place on Monday evenings.

"I will provide the wine if y'all provide the snacks."

"Oh fun! "Ruby Jean clapped your hands together.

"Okay well it's settled then. Next Monday my place around 7:00 pm. Let's start with the book 'Boogeyman's Daughter' by KY Lewis. It's a psychological Thriller.

"Yay, that's on my reading list!" Ruby Jean blurted.

"I love psychological thrillers."

"This is going to be so much fun!" Ruby Jean clapped her hands again.

"Ruby Jean girl, you are goofy, but I love it!" Lisa commented.

I turned to look out the window and I saw Cheyenne's car explode.

I thought to myself, "Oh my word, did that really just happen?" Everyone started to freak out.

"Cheyenne, that was your car!" I panicked.

Cheyenne started to get up.

"No! Cheyenne, you can't go out there, it's dangerous!" She sat back down and started to cry.

Lisa got up and hugged her while I called Jay.

Ruby Jean started to cry also. Lisa stood in between them and rubbed their backs for comfort.

I'm not the most touchy feely person except with Jay. but I'm getting better. So I take them both by the hand.

"Ladies everything will be ok. Jay is on his way."

We heard an ambulance a minute later and it pulled in. It was parked in the back area. Within 5 minutes Jay and Billy pulled up and Jay got out to talk to the paramedics.

Soon after that the bomb squad pulled up. Jay spoke to the head guy. They had a canine sniff around for any more bombs. Unfortunately they found a victim in front of the car next to Cheyenne's car.

Another car exploded on the other side of the parking lot. The K9 had not gotten to that side yet. No one was hurt on that side.

"He's going to kill us all!" Ruby Jean yelled.

"Don't get worked up and start yelling Ruby Jean you're going to cause more panic!" I asserted.

17

It had been 20 minutes when Jay came into the coffee shop.

"I need everyone to listen up. At this time I need everyone to leave the property so the K9 dogs can do their job. I want everyone to form a single file line and go out the door calmly one at a time. Thank you for your patience!"

People started to line up to go out. I pulled Jay aside.

"Jay, do you think there are more bombs?"

"Probably not my love. The bombs would have already gone off. This is just precautionary and routine after a bomb or a bomb threat. I need you to go home." When I stepped out of the coffee shop I saw Billy, Tommy and Glenn holding doors open to the other businesses. There were people in single files going out of the businesses.

As Cheyenne and I were leaving I shook my head in disgust. I saw them loading the victim up. When Cheyenne saw the victim she started to shake and cry again. I took her to the shop to get her mind off things. She got to see how things were coming along with the shop. Unfortunately we got a group text from Unknown.

"I hope everyone enjoyed the show. Especially you Cheyenne! BOOM!"

"Do not respond!" Jay text.

"Oh come on Queen bee, you know you want to."

"Okay psycho, you will get what's coming to you. Romans 12:19 vengeance is mine, I will repay says the Lord! You need to watch your back, creep!" I texted.

"Get em Summer!" Ruby Jean text.

"Enough!" Jay text.

"Hey Mary Poppins bring your umbrella and mess with me. Coward messing with a bunch of women. Boy, you ain't got no sense about you. You must have been dropped on your head as a baby. It seems to me you're a sissy boy. Come get some. I'll be the one with the shotgun pointed at you. Between you and me, we know who can shoot and who can't, loser!" Jonathan text.

"You've got a lot to say country bumpkin. I've got your number and it's just a matter of time!" -Unknown text.

"Well I hope you've been practicing because those three shots you fired at me, tell me you're an amateur. I'm sure your toy gun has come in handy with you trying to practice! Sissy boy. Did your mama teach you to shoot?"

"Enough Jonathan, now!" Jay text.

"It's okay, Jay! Country bumpkin and his dingbat have it coming."-Unknown

"No more texting, I'm trying to protect everyone!"-Jay

"It's pitiful Jay. You can't even get your own people to listen to you, how are you going to protect them?"- Unknown text.

I TOOK CHEYENNE BACK to my place and we sat down on the sofa. We decided to watch movies to get our minds off things. At 5:00 p.m. Jay came over and we all went to dinner. The rest of the week seemed to go smoothly.

MONDAY EVENING WE ALL went to Lisa's place. She had a male cat named Patches. He was sweet and friendly.

"So ladies, how far did you get in the book?" She asked as she gave each one of us a glass of wine.

"Molly had just left the prison where I left off." Cheyenne commented.

I shook my head in agreement.

"I stopped where she was looking Jackson's information up." Lisa said.

" I only got to the prologue. I'm kind of a slow reader. The toy chest is spooky!" Ruby Jean replied.

"It sure was! Rick is obviously scary because he's a serial killer; but I'll tell you that Jackson he's odd. I'm not sure what to make of him. I wonder if he's going to be a problem for Molly?" Lisa spoke up.

"I was wondering myself. I found Molly to be a little bit rough around the edges. At this point in time I can't tell if she's mad at life or if she's just guarded because of what she went through?" I questioned.

BACK AT MY CONDO ALL is quiet except for Augie snoring. Mr Stew had had enough of the snoring. He slowly jumped off his cat post and jumped on the sofa. Augie was on the floor, tongue hanging out the side of his mouth and his lips flapping every time his loud snore passed through his lips.

Mr. Stew stared at Augie for a moment and thought to himself, "Look at that fur ball. His tongues hanging out and he's drooling. Such an awful noise he makes. He makes my fur crawl!"

Mr. Stew reached down and slapped Augie on the head three times. Augie jumped up and saw Mr. Stew on the couch glaring at him. Augie wagged his tail at Mr.Stew.

Mr. Stew went back and jumped up on his post and thought, "that furball is an idiot. He's wagging his tail after I slapped him!"

They both heard the door open. I walked in and hung my keys up. I sat down and watched some video on my phone of when I was gone tonight. I saw what Mr.Stew did and shook my head.

I was tired and decided to go to bed. I have to be at the shop tomorrow. I will get to the coffee shop at about 7:30 to meet the girls. Everyone pretty much has a set schedule so as far as a shop goes things are looking up. I fell asleep thinking about it.

18

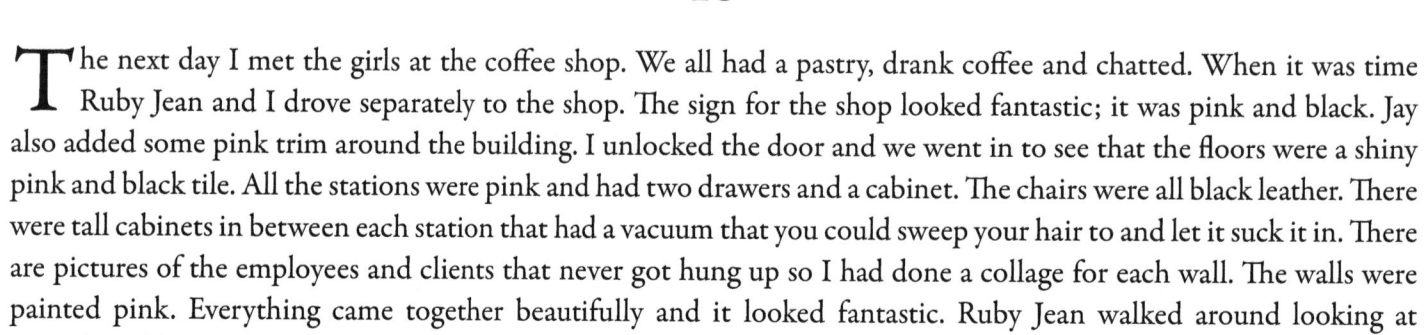

The next day I met the girls at the coffee shop. We all had a pastry, drank coffee and chatted. When it was time Ruby Jean and I drove separately to the shop. The sign for the shop looked fantastic; it was pink and black. Jay also added some pink trim around the building. I unlocked the door and we went in to see that the floors were a shiny pink and black tile. All the stations were pink and had two drawers and a cabinet. The chairs were all black leather. There were tall cabinets in between each station that had a vacuum that you could sweep your hair to and let it suck it in. There are pictures of the employees and clients that never got hung up so I had done a collage for each wall. The walls were painted pink. Everything came together beautifully and it looked fantastic. Ruby Jean walked around looking at everything like a kid in a candy store. She was so excited. Wyatt walked in and his mouth dropped open.

Bailey came in behind him. "I love it, Summer!

"Wow, I have to take a pic and send it to Beverly. She knew you'd do something great with the shop!" Wyatt stated.

He kept taking pictures everywhere and smiling while shaking his head.

"This is beautiful!" Bailey's eyes were wide open.

"Thank you both!" I said.

Our first couple of clients walked in. One was my aunt Betty.

"Oh summer honey, this is beautiful!" "Thank you Aunt Betty, I love it too!"

She sat down at my station. "So are the prices still the same?"

"Everyone's service will be up to the stylist to decide. Obviously if the stylist is way overcharging I will say something. Since you're my aunt you get free services."

"Well that is very kind of you summer. Finally something good has happened since Rhett died. I sure do miss him!"

"I know you do, so do I."

"I heard there was a victim of the car bombing. Summer, don't you go to that coffee shop?"

"Yes I sent flowers to the victim's family. Cheyenne's car was one of the cars. Thankfully she wasn't in it and she now has a new car."

"Oh my Summer thank goodness she wasn't in it. How awful!"

"Yes she was in the coffee shop with us thankfully!" Aunt Betty shook her head in agreement.

Ruby Jean was done setting up.

"Okay Sarah, are you ready to become beautiful?"

Sarah laughed. "Ruby Jean, I've been waiting for that all my life!"

We all laughed.

"Bailey, shadow Ruby Jean for the highlights. It would be a good learning experience for you." I mentioned.

"Come on over girly!" Ruby Jean smiled at Bailey.

Bailey smiled back and stood against the wall behind Ruby Jean. She could see everything but she wouldn't be in the way standing there.

"Ruby Jean can we make my highlights brighter?"

"We sure can, fun!"

Wyatt looked out the glass doors and saw Jonathan sitting there in his truck.

"Ruby Jean, why is Jonathan just sitting as a truck out there?"

" Oh well, Jonathan's just making sure I don't get blown up."

"So he's just going to sit down in his truck all day?"

"Yep, that's his plan."

Wyatt smirked at me and walked back over to the front desk.

"Okay Bailey let's go create her formula."

My Aunt Betty spoke up. "How is her boyfriend sitting in his truck all day going to stop a bomb? That makes no sense!"

Wyatt spoke up. "Her boyfriend Jonathan is just as dingy as she is."

"Wyatt , keep it down, you'll hurt her feelings if she hears you say that."

"Well, Summer, am I wrong?

"No but that's one of the things we love about her."

Wyatt half smiled at me. "True." I finished up with my aunt.

"Summer sweetie, we'll have to get lunch real soon."

" I would love that."

"Great! Thank you for my beautiful haircut. I'll see you later honey."

3:00 p.m. was shift change and Cheyenne and Lisa came in. Beau is doing second shift but he's always running late.

"Wow, this place looks amazing!" Lisa smiled.

Cheyenne looked around with a smile on her face.

"It sure does!"

"Summer I'm just going to stay over because Beverly is out of town visiting her sister in Alabama."

"Ok, no problem Wyatt!"

"Hey y'all!" Beau came through the doors.

"What's up with Jonathan just sitting in his truck out there?"

"Beau, he's just making sure I don't get blown up."

" Ok, so he's Superman for the day and he can stop a bomb, cool!" Wyatt chuckled.

I tried very hard not to chuckle.

Beau looked around.

"By the way, Summer, the place looks fabulous! " Thank you all so much for loving the changes!" This actually made me tear up a little bit.

"Thank you all for the support."

I WENT HOME AND CLEANED my condo. I've been slacking the last few weeks. Jay came over with some Chinese food.

"Hello my love!"

"Hi!" I gave him a kiss.

We sat on the sofa. I put his box of Chinese out on the coffee table. Then I took mine out of the bag.

I noticed something attached to it. It was a string dangling that looked like it was coming from the inside of the box. I pulled on it and a diamond ring popped out.

It was gorgeous!

"Jay!" I looked at him.

"Summer, you are the love of my life. I will ask you again and again if you will marry me until you say yes. I don't want to be without you ever again!"

I teared up. "Yes Jay a million times over, yes. I should have married you the first time you proposed. But I was scared. I'm sorry you're the love of my life and I can't imagine being without you!"

"I wasn't sure about the timing considering everything. Something inside me kept telling me I need to just go ahead and ask you to marry me."

"The timing is just perfect Jay, just perfect!" I gave him a warm kiss and hug.

19

The next morning I met the ladies at the coffee shop at 8:30 to have plenty of time.. The grand reopening of my shop is at 9:00 am. 10:00 a.m. will be the regular time for the shop to open.

As soon as I sat down Lisa noticed my ring.

"Summer that ring is gorgeous, congratulations!"

"Thank you!"

"It is beautiful and it's about time!" "It's so pretty. OH GOODIE!"

Ruby Jean clapped her hands.

I smile." Thanks a lot ladies. It will be a small ceremony in three months. June 10th at 12:30 at our church I spoke to the pastor last night."

"Which one of us is your bridesmaid?" Ruby Jean asked in a child like manner.

"You and Cheyenne, silly."

"Sorry Lisa."

"No girl please, I just want to be invited to your wedding. I'm good!"

"You're absolutely invited to the wedding."

"Ruby Jean, when is your wedding?" I asked.

"Oh, well, we can't decide. I need a few years. I want a big princess wedding!" We all shook our heads in agreement because that was so fitting for her.

CHEYENNE AND I LEFT separately and headed to the shop. Cheyenne was ahead of me. Out of nowhere a black truck knocked into my back bumper. They ran me into the ditch. I cannot see who was driving. They sped up to go around Cheyenne.

Cheyenne's heart raced and she started to shake because she knew it was the killer.

She stopped and pulled over. She got out and ran to my car.

"Are you okay Summer?"

"I'm okay. My tire is flat and my back bumper is a little dented!" We were standing behind my car.

A police cruiser came down the street. It was Tommy and he pulled over.

"Hey ladies, are you okay?"

"That psycho ran Summer into the ditch!"

"I have a flat tire and a dent in my bumper!"

"Oh yeah I see that. Ladies hop in the cruiser and I'll take you back to the station because a report needs to be filed. Summer, I'll come fix your tire and have it brought back to the station."

"Thanks Tommy!" I smiled.

When we got to the station and went in we saw Jay was sitting at his desk. We went and sat in front of his desk.

"Everything okay ladies?"

"No, that creeper ran Summer off the road into a ditch! "Cheyenne's voice trembled. I was starting to get a migraine and I could feel my blood pressure shooting up. My face must have been red because Jay asked Tommy to get us some water.

He went and got us two bottles of water. He's a good guy.

"My love, drink some more water, your face is still red."

I drank more water and then I took a deep breath and started to calm down.

"Did either of you get a look at the driver or what they were driving?" " No!" we both said.

"I did see it was a black truck!"

Cheyenne shook her head in agreement.

My voice trembled. " It happened so fast I didn't even see the license plate."

" Nor did I."

Jay had let out a sigh of concern.

"Summer, how's your car?"

"I have a flat tire that Tommy is going to fix and a dent in the bumper. It's not bad."

Jay rubbed his chin. "We need to figure out how to trap this guy!" Billy walked in. "Tommy told me what happened. Are you ladies okay?" We both shook our heads yes.

"It was a black truck," Jay pointed out.

" Oh man you're kidding! Well that's going to take a while to narrow down. There's a lot of black trucks from here to Mayville and Sanford. That includes myself, Glenn, Charlie and you Jay."

"Who is Charlie?" I asked.

"He's the new guy on the night shift that works with Glen."

Tommy walked in. "Hey, I have a black truck also."

"Oh man that's right, how did I miss that! Do you ladies remember anything that stood out, maybe like a decal or a sticker?" I shook my head no.

"I was thinking we need to trap him somehow?" Jay commented.

I got distracted for a moment because Wyatt texted me.

"Are you and Cheyenne okay, where are you?"

"We won't be in today. I'll fill you in later."

"No problem. I can do some services today. Lisa is coming in early at 1:00 p.m. Can I let Bailey cut some hair if I check behind her?"

"Sure, go ahead."

" Cool Summer thanks, talk to you later."

Everyone remained quiet for a minute longer.

"So who are we going to use for bait? He has to be baited!" Billy blurted out.

We all got quiet again.

Tommy spoke up. "Let me put my two cents in. It has to be summer, Cheyenne or Jonathan. He has gone after them the most. You can't be the babe because he has you where he wants you right now. You're the leader of the pack and he wants to see you squirm. It can't be Jonathan, he's too much of a hot head."

"I don't want to do it, he might kidnap me again!"Cheyenne's voice trembled.

"I guess that leaves me. It's ok. I survived the showdown with my evil sister." I took a deep breath. Jay looked at all of us.

He rubbed his chin and said, " I'm not sure it's such a good idea to send you in Summer. First of all, you're my fiance. Secondly you're a citizen."

"Congrats!" Billy and Tommy both said.

"It's about time. You two have been together forever, except for your little break." Billy chuckled.

Cheyenne spoke up. "So have we Billy, except for our little break." Billy rolled his eyes.

"Anyways, we could be waiting in the cruisers nearby." Billy suggested.

"All right, when he texts again Summer will challenge him to a meeting. You need to have your gun with you! And it's important that you follow my instructions!" Jay demanded.

I could tell Jay's left jaw was tightening up. He was trying to keep his cool.

"Billy can take you ladies home. Summer we'll talk later." I could hear the frustration in Jay's voice.

20

Billy dropped me off and he and Cheyenne went to her place. They seem to be arguing a lot lately. It's just like old times. They were always arguing in high school. When Cheyenne and Billy went into her place they met her dog Jack. He looked at Billy's hand and wagged his tail.

" German shepherds are the best!" Billy scratched behind Jack's ears.

"I know I'm so thankful for him."

"All right I have to head back to work."

He gave her a quick kiss and headed out

I WAS TAKING A NAP when a group text came through from Unknown. "Hey Queen bee is your car ok? I will run you into a tree next time!" Everyone was reading the group text.

Wyatt shook his head in disgust. "Well that explains why they didn't come into work. What a creep!"

"Beau answered. "Well you certainly don't know how to get a life! Just look at you pitiful!"

"You would be wise to stop talking, Beau!"- Unknown

"If you're such a scary psycho then why don't you meet me at Riker amusement park in Sanford. You know the amusement park I got shut down 5 years ago." I text.

"Do you really want to die tonight queen bee? Don't tempt me!" "I'm challenging you, creep!" I gritted my teeth.

"Ha-ha, fine 10 pm I want it nice and dark. It'll be fun to play cat and mouse with you!"

Jay sent a mass text to all of us. "No more responding to this idiot!" Jay then called me.

"Summer I will be at your place at 9:30. Tommy, Billy, Glenn and I will follow you."

"Sounds good, but you all need to stay out of sight." "Don't worry we will. Love you." He hung up.

I stayed busy around my place until it was time to go. I was trying to calm my nerves.

Billy unlocked my door and came in.

"You need a safe word that everyone knows. The word will be "blue."

"Okay blue it is."

He stuck a tiny microphone behind my ear. It looked a little bit like a hearing aid but it stuck to my skin.

" I will be able to hear everything that's going on."

I loved Mr. Stew and Augie then locked up. I headed to my car. It was weird seeing so many black trucks at once.

I hopped in my car and took off with the four black trucks behind me. It took about 20 minutes to get there. All the guys parked in different spots surrounding the park. They concealed themselves. Now they would be talking through text. The radios that they usually talk through are in the cruisers. They chose to drive their trucks because cruisers would draw attention.

I pulled into the parking lot and no cars were around. I got out and climbed the fence. I had my gun tucked in the back of my jeans and I also had a flashlight. I walked about 10 ft. in when a pole with the light popped on. There he was dressed in all black. He had a ski mask on and gloves. I pulled my gun out and pointed towards him.

"Hello Summer, we finally got to meet in person. So are you ready to play cat and mouse?"

"Do you mean I'm the cat and you're the mouse weirdo?"

"No Summer, I'm the cat and you're the mouse!" he said smugly.

I stepped a few feet back. Then I ran to the left and hid under one of the tables.

"Come on out queen bee where's your stinger? Haha!"

I could see the bottom of his legs. He walked past the table but then stopped. He turned around and came to the table pulling the cloth up.

"BOO!" He was right in my face.

I picked up some dirt and threw dirt in his face. That just gave me time to get out from underneath the table and run.

Jay was thinking to himself, "I want to go in there now. I don't even know where they are at. Come on Summer, say where you're located." Jay could hear me but I couldn't hear him.

He had gotten the dirt out of his eyes and was on the hunt for Summer again.

" Summer, that wasn't nice. I think you'll get an extra punishment for that,witch!" I wanted to run back to the fence and climb it but I knew he would see me and shoot at me. So I ran into the fun house. The lights came on and it was bright. I started to walk around and it got confusing. Then I saw the killer to my left. I fired my gun and that mirror shattered. I could hear him chuckling.

"Oh come on Queen Bee you can do better than that. Aren't you having fun yet, I am. You should know better than to challenge me!" "What did I do to you? What do you want from me psycho?" I was starting to get dizzy.

I could feel and hear him whisper into my ear.

"To mess with you a while longer and then take your life!"

Jay heard that and he started on his way over. He could hear the mirror being shattered so he knew I was in the fun house.

Turning around and firing my gun again shattered another mirror. The creep chuckled loudly. Then I heard Jay yell for me.

I screamed, "blue, blue, blue!"

Jay was at my side within seconds. He picked me up and carried me outside. He set me on the steps.

We heard someone chuckle in the distance.

"You're never going to catch me!"

Jay drew his gun and headed towards the voice.

I heard shots fired and then silence. A few minutes later Jay was back with Tommy and Glen.

"Where is Billy?" Tommy asked.

"I told him to go check on Cheyenne. She has not answered her phone all evening.

I want to scour this place one more time. Summer you go home and get some rest.

BILLY UNLOCKED CHEYENNE'S door and was met with Jack. Cheyenne was on the sofa watching TV.

"Hey, why aren't you answering your phone? You had Jay and I worried."

"I'm sorry I did not hear it ring."

Cheyenne looked around but she could not find her phone.

"I can't find it Billy. Will you go look at my car for it? I'm tired."

Billy went out to Cheyenne's car. A few minutes later he came back in.

"I found it under your seat."

All the messages from Billy and Jay were on it.

"Woman, try to be more careful!"

"I said I was sorry!" She rolled her eyes. "I guess I'll head out since you're in a mood!" He shook his head.

"I told you I'm just tired, sorry."

Billy headed out after texting Jay.

I WAS AT HOME AND RESTING on the sofa when I got a text.

"I really enjoyed our encounter tonight. When I saw you head into the fun house I knew it was going to be an exciting night. I could smell your fear. Until next time queen bee!"

I did not reply.

I was really spooked he got that close to me. I really need to be on my toes. The next day I went into work at 3:00 p.m. Lisa and Bailey were there to work the evening shift with me.

"Hey ladies." They both smiled and said hello.

"Bailey, how do you feel things are coming along?"

"I'm getting better every day."

"Good, I will check on your haircut tonight. I will turn you loose after that. Only for haircuts though!" Bailey gave me an eager smile.

Lisa spoke up. "I have to ask how did it go last night? Cheyenne told me where you were going"

" It was awful and he is still not caught."

" I'll tell you what girl when I saw you were going to meet him my heart skipped a beat! I'm trying to remain quiet to stay off his radar."

"Lisa, I understand. We'll go out to our cars together this evening. When you get home watch your surroundings that means you as well Bailey."

"Yeah he really is scary. I've never had somebody want to hurt me!"Bailey commented.

"I wish I could say the same." I responded.

22

3 months later and we haven't really heard anything from the psycho. It's my wedding day. With help I was able to throw everything together.

I was in one of the back rooms in the church getting ready. Cheyenne and Ruby Jean look beautiful in their pink dresses. I let them go ahead and pick them out themselves. They stepped out of the room to give me privacy with my Aunt Betty.

"Summer you look so beautiful!"

She started to tear up. Then she put a locket out of her purse.

She put it on me. "This belonged to your great-grandmother."

"I don't know what to say, it's so beautiful. Thank you Aunt Betty!"

"I'm so thankful you're here to see me get married."

"Your mother would be so proud of you. Aunt Lucy is here as well. Your mother would want both her sisters here."

I started to tear up. I can see a lot of my mom in my Aunt Betty.

"Thank you Aunt Betty."

She gave me a hug. "I will let you have some privacy now Summer."

I was putting on my shoes when the door opened. There stood the killer once again in all black with the ski mask and gloves. My heart was in my throat. I was paralyzed with fear. I couldn't move or scream. He walked over to me and shot a needle in my arm. Everything faded to black.

The killer got me out of the building and into the trunk of his car. That's right I said car. He drove a car this time.

20 minutes later Cheyenne was looking for Billy. She popped her head around the back of the church and saw Billy smoking in the back parking lot.

She walked up to him. "Really Billy, I told you to stop that nasty habit. Especially on church grounds.

"Why are you always such a judgmental woman! It's just one cigarette.

"I'm not going to kiss you anymore until you stop this habit!" She started to walk away.

"Oh come on little lady don't be like that!"

Billy rolled his eyes and smirked, then shook his head. He put the cigarette out and went inside. He sat down next to Cheyenne. He put his arm around her and she refused to look at him. She looked at the time on the clock that was on the wall to the left.

She leaned into Ruby Jean and whispered, " It's time." They got up and headed into the hall.

I WOKE UP. MY EYES were hazy and my mouth was taped up. My feet and hands are bound. I had no strength in my body, not even to lift my head. Panic washed over me which made me feel nauseous. I told myself I needed to get angry instead of being scared. I refuse to let this be the end for me.

CHEYENNE AND RUBY JEAN came to the room to get me and I was gone. There were no signs of struggle in the room. Cheyenne, Ruby Jean, Billy, Jonathan, Tommy and Glen looked all over for me.

Lisa and Bailey came into the hall. And Betty was right behind them.

"Is everything okay kids?" Aunt Betty asked with a shaky voice.

"What's going on! "Jay said as he came up behind everyone.

"Well, um, we can't find Summer," Billy answered.

"Has anyone called her phone? "Jay had concern in his voice.

Billy called Summers' phone and it could be heard ringing in the room.

Jay booked his head into the sanctuary and waved to Pastor Mason to come out into the hall.

"Is everything okay? "Pastor Mason asked.

"No Summer is missing. I need to see the footage from the last 2 hours." Jay insisted.

Pastor took Jay and Billy to the camera room.

"We have cameras in every room except for the bathrooms and my office. I counsel people in my office so I don't want a camera in there! The room Summer was in does have a bathroom. Is it possible she's in there?"

" She is not. It's been checked." Billy answered.

Pastor Mason pulled up the last 2 hours.

"Go ahead and take over Billy."

Pastor Mason got up and Billy sat down and started to fast forward until he reached the point that I was taken.

"Oh no, we need heavy prayer!" Pastor Mason said as he put his hand over his chest.

"Why isn't she moving! Billy asked.

"Because she's frozen with fear. She probably couldn't yell for help either. "Jay answered, annoyed.

" I'm going to go and make an announcement for everyone to go home." "Please do. Thank you Pastor." Jay replied.

Billy and Jay came out of the room.

"Okay everyone the psychopath has Summer. We saw the video!"

"He has my Summer! Oh, I don't feel good. My beautiful Summer!" Aunt Betty started to cry.

"Ladies please take Betty home and go home after that. "Jay was stern.

"Jay man, I want to help?" Jonathan said.

" Ok Jonathan, you can help Tommy go around the neighborhood. Talk to every house asking if anyone has seen anything, thanks. Billy, you and I can head to that gas station where we picked up Cheyenne. Maybe somebody saw something out there."

They all headed out and I'm still in the trunk. I fell asleep from being so worn out.

Hours later the trunk door was yanked open and caught me by surprise. It was very dark out and it seemed to be very late.

"I bet that air feels good after being in the trunk for 10 hours. Look at you all sweaty, makeup runny down your face and your dress is torn. You're a pitiful sight." He chuckled as he shoved a needle into my arm. Everything went black again. No one was able to get any information. I'm nowhere to be found. Jay has been going out of his mind trying to find me!

The killer sent a group text.

"The queen bee is safe for now. This is the second time I've outsmarted her. W!" Unknown text.

" No one else is to respond. When I find you man, I'm going to kill you. Taking my sister was your first mistake. Summer is your second mistake. Be ready for me and my army will find you. We will finish you. Do not harm one hair on Summer's head. Enough said!"

That gave the killer a little bit of a chill down his spine. Then he got angry. Now I will make it all about Summer!

23

I woke up again in a room I wasn't familiar with. I was lying on a bed. The room looked exactly like the one Cheyenne described.

My feet and hands are not bound any longer and I have strength in my body again. The killer unlocked the door and came into the room. He had a tray of food and a drink. He sat on the bed. He went to the window because he noticed a piece of the black paper was coming up in the corner. While he was fixing that I took everything off the tray. The tray felt pretty thick. I got off the bed and swung as hard as I could whacking him in the back of the head. He quickly turned around and I whacked him again across the face. It knocked him out. I shut the door and locked it behind me. I found my way out of the house as quickly as I could. I started running up the trail that the car goes on until I hit the main road. The first car that passed I flagged down. It happened to be a young woman.

"Are you okay Miss?"

"Can you take me to the nearest gas station? I was kidnapped!"

"I'm sorry to hear that, was it your wedding day?"

"Yes, my dress is all torn and ruined."

The lady dropped me off at the nearest gas station which happened to be the one that Cheyenne was picked up at.

"Thank you so much!"

"No problem, are you sure you don't want me to take you to the police station?"

"No, this is good, thank you."

The cashier let me use his phone and I called Jay who was frantic.

"Ma'am, another lady was kidnapped not too long ago and she needed to use the phone here. She's just a little petite thing." the cashier said.

"Yes she's one of my best friends!"

"Oh I see y'all got some strange things going on in your town!"

I shook my head in agreement. It took a while but Jay pulled up into the gas station parking lot. He jumped out of his cruiser and gave me a warm hug.

"Oh my love I was so worried!"

It felt good to be back in his arms. We headed back to Blue Ash.

"Were you able to get a look at his face this time?"

"No, I wasn't able to see his face because the ski mask was on. I whacked him in the head and in the face with a thick tray. I bet he'll have a headache when he wakes up, ha-ha! I'm so angry that our wedding was ruined!"

"Let's not worry about that. We will get married when the time is right."

"Has anyone checked on my Aunt? She must be worried sick?"

" Ruby Jean and Cheyenne brought her home yesterday."

" The locket that Aunt Betty gave me was gone. It belonged to my great grandma." We got to my place and he walked me in. Augie and Mr. Stew were at the door to greet us.

" Mr. Stew meowed and thought to himself, "Oh good mommy's home I know I lost 5 lb. I'm starving."

I fed and loved them and then I got in the shower. I changed clothes. We went to the police station so he could fill out a report.

Billy, Tommy and Glen were off because it was Sunday.

I got to meet Charlie He popped his head in the door of Jay's office .

"You must be the famous Summer Meadows?" "That would be me." I smiled.

I got a creepy vibe from him.

His wife came in and headed to the office.

"Honey, you left your phone in the car."

" Oh snap, I sure did."

"Thanks Babe. This is my wife Cassandra."

Right then I noticed the locket she was wearing because it was the one my Aunt gave Me .

I swallowed hard and said "what a beautiful locket!"

"Oh thanks, Charlie found it in the church parking lot yesterday at your wedding. I'm so glad you are ok !"

"I will walk you out Babe."

They left the office and then the building.

"Jay, that's the locket my aunt gave me!"

"Are you sure Summer?"

"Yes, it had a tiny rose on the front!"

Jay paused for a moment and took a deep breath.

"Summer, I never invited him to the wedding. Ok, let's just lay low and play it cool until I can figure out what to do."

" Ok, I agree we need more proof. He does give me a creepy vibe. Can you run a better background check on him?"

"Yes I can ask Agent Adams to do an FBI check on him. The check I have only goes back five years ."

" Oh ok . Hey, we need to check on my aunt. I will send a mass text that I'm back safely."

" Sounds good, let's get out of here ."

As we pulled up to my aunt's house I noticed there were no lights on. Her car was in the driveway. I had a key so I unlocked the door and we went on in. It was hot inside and a terrible odor was in the air.

"Summer, go wait outside!"

I went outside and waited on the porch.

Jay had his gun drawn and his flashlight on.

He looked around the front room and then went into the kitchen. There he saw Betty lying on the floor. It was obvious she was gone.

"Oh you're kidding me!" Jay shook his head in anger .

He came back outside.

"I'm sorry Summer!"

"No, not my sweet Aunt Betty!"

I started to cry. He hugged me and told me he was going to take me home.

I STAYED OUT OF WORK for the next two weeks. The whole crew did a great job running the shop. Especially Wyatt. The funeral for my Aunt Betty was beautiful.

IT'S BEEN A FEW MONTHS since my Aunt Betty's death. Three hairs came back from the crime scene. They belong to Charlie. He was arrested. Of course he claims those hairs were from when he was working the case.

So why was he at the wedding when he wasn't invited? Why didn't he ask around to see if somebody had lost my locket? It just seems strange. Now I will say that things have been quiet since he's been arrested. Charlie went to school with us. We didn't recognize him because he went by his first name Allen back then. Cheyenne and I saw him kissing a female teacher. We told the principal and he was sent away and the teacher was fired. Everyone thinks he's the killer, but is he?

THE END

If you enjoyed this book please leave a review on Amazon and Good Reads . Book three will be the final book in this series.